我和我的翻译

我得重下海去

黄杲炘译诗自选集

黄杲炘 译著

中国出版集团
中译出版社

丛书编辑说明

"我和我的翻译"系列丛书由罗选民教授担任主编,第一辑遴选了12位当代中国有影响力的翻译家,以自选集的方式,收录其代表译著篇目或选段,涵盖小说、散文、诗歌等多种体裁,涉及英、德、法、日、西、俄等多个语种,集中展示了当代翻译家群体的译著成果。

丛书篇目及选段大多是翻译家已出版的经典作品,长期受到读者的喜爱和追捧。每本书的译者不仅是知名翻译家,还是高校教授翻译、文学课程的名师,对译文的把握、注释、点评精辟到位。因此,这套丛书不仅具有一定的文学价值,同样具有较高的收藏价值和研究价值,是翻译研究的宝贵历史语料,也可作为外语学习者研习翻译的资料使用,更值得文学爱好者品读、体会。

书稿根据译者亲自校订的最后版本排印,经过了精心的编辑,主要包括以下几方面的处理:

一、译者及篇目信息

1. 丛书的每个分册各集中展示一位翻译家的译著面貌,文前增添翻译家自序,由译者本人对自己的翻译理念、自选作品的背景和脉络等进行总体介绍。

2. 每篇文章都注明了出处，读者可依据兴趣溯源阅读。

3. 根据各位翻译家对篇目的编排，章前或作品前增添导读，由译者自拟，解析原著内容和写作特色，帮助读者更深入、全面地理解文本。

4. 书后附译著版本目录，方便读者查找对照、进行延伸阅读。

二、译文注释与修改

1. 在译文必要的位置增加脚注，对一些陌生的表述，如人名、地名、书名等做了必要的注释，有助于读者理解术语的文化背景及历史渊源。

2. 遵照各位翻译家的意愿，书中有的拼写仍然保留了古英语的写法和格式，原汁原味。

3. 诗歌部分，考虑其翻译的特殊性，可探讨空间较大，并且具有英文阅读能力的读者较多，特将原文为英文的诗歌，以中英双语形式呈现。

由于编辑水平有限，书稿中肯定还存在一些不足之处，望各位读者批评指正。

丛书总序

百年征程育华章　薪火相传谱新曲

翻译是文化之托命者。翻译盛，其文化盛，如连绵数千年的中华文明；翻译衰，则其文化衰，如早已隔世、销声匿迹的墨西哥玛雅文化、印度佛教文化。文化传承，犹如薪火相传；静止、封闭的文化，犹如一潭死水，以枯竭告终。

翻译是思想的融通、心智的默契、语言的传神。化腐朽为神奇是翻译的文学性体现，化作利器来改造社会与文化乃是翻译的社会性体现。前者主要关注人性陶冶和慰藉人生，个性飞扬，神采怡然；后者主要关注社会变革和教化人伦，语言达旨，表述严谨。在清末的两类译者中，代表性人物是林纾和严复。林纾与他人合作翻译了180余部西洋小说，其中不少为世界名著，尤其译著《茶花女》赢得严复如下称赞："孤山处士音琅琅，皂袍演说常登堂。可怜一卷茶花女，断尽支那荡子肠。"[1] 严复则翻译了大量西方的社会学、政治学、经济学、法学、哲学等方面的著作，是中国近代重要的思想启蒙家，其译著《天演论》影响尤为深远。该书前言中提出的"信、达、雅"翻译标准对后世影响

1　严复，《甲辰出都呈同里诸公》。

很大。严复本人也因此被誉为中国近代史上向西方国家寻找真理的"先进的中国人"之一。

此后百余年,我国出现了一大批优秀文学翻译家,如鲁迅、朱生豪、傅雷、梁实秋、罗念生、季羡林、孙大雨、卞之琳、查良铮、杨绛等。他们的翻译作品影响了一个时代,影响了一批中国现当代文学家,有力地推动了中国现当代文学的创新与发展。

余光中先生有一段关于译者的描述:"译者未必有学者的权威,或是作家的声誉,但其影响未必较小,甚或更大。译者日与伟大的心灵为伍,见贤思齐,当其意会笔到,每能超凡入圣,成为神之巫师,天才之代言人。此乃寂寞译者独享之特权。"[1] 我以为,这是对译者最客观、最慷慨的赞许,尽管今天像余先生笔下的那类译者已不多见。

有人描述过今天翻译界的现状:能做翻译的人不做翻译,不做翻译的人在做翻译研究。这个说法不全对,但确实也是一个存在的现象。我们只要翻阅一些已出版的译书就不难发现词不达意、曲解原文的现象。这是翻译界的一个怪圈,是一种不健康的翻译生态现象。

作为学者、译者、出版者,我们无法做到很多,但塑造翻译经典、提倡阅读翻译经典是我们应该可以做到的事情,这是我们编辑这套丛书的初衷。编辑这套丛书也受到了漓江出版社的启发。该社曾开发"当代著名翻译家精品丛书",出了一辑就停止了,实为遗憾。

本丛书遴选了12位当代有影响力的翻译家,以自选集的形式,收录译文、译著片段,集中反映了当代翻译家所取得的成绩。收录译文

1　余光中,《余光中谈翻译》,中国对外翻译出版公司,2002。

基本上是外译中，目前，外国语种包括英语、俄语、法语、德语、西班牙语、日语。每本书均有丛书总序、译者自序，每部分前有译者按语或导读。译丛尤其推崇首译佳作。本次入选的译本丛书可以视为当代知名翻译家群体成果的集中展示，是一种难得的文化记忆，可供文学和翻译爱好者欣赏与学习。

如今，适逢中国面临百年未有之大变局之际，中译出版社的领导高度重视，支持出版"我和我的翻译"丛书，可以视为翻译出版的薪火相传，以精选译文为依托，讲述中国翻译的故事，推动优秀文化的世界传播！

罗选民

2021 年 7 月 1 日于广西大学镜湖斋

译者自序
译路上的管窥过客[1]

我本准备2016年告别翻译,偏偏各种机缘纷至沓来,让我的旧译新著几乎全部出笼。做好24本书,眼力已山穷水尽,于是写了《告别翻译》,发表在《东方翻译》2019年第5期,算是正式结束。想不到过了半年,罗选民教授和胡晓凯女士邀我做英汉对照的"自选集"。我虽然最喜欢译诗以英汉对照方式出版,多年前收进两本拙译的中译出版社"一百丛书"也留下了良好印象,而且做"自选集"材料现成,可不用花多少眼力,当时心里却很矛盾。但考虑下来还是决定做。因为拙译单是译诗就在六万行以上,也确实应当做个供一般浏览的"精简本"。根据这套"自选集"体例,书前要介绍翻译经历,下面就做一回顾,其间的五味杂陈似乎还不多见。

---

[1] 本文曾发表于《东方翻译》2020年第4期,有改动。

一

半个多世纪前,我在人生的峡谷中偶遇英诗,当时眼睛的情况也让我犹如身在峡谷,因为视网膜病变已使我丧失了绝大部分视野,只有中心视力尚未受很大影响,形成了"管状视野"。或许正是这情况,使我的兴趣集中于眼前的英诗,总之,我读着读着就喜欢了,随后试着翻译翻译,更喜欢了,就以译诗自娱自励并通过译诗自学。在摸索格律诗翻译之道的过程中,我有过多种尝试。最早当然是按通常做法,一律译成自由诗,或在此基础上随便用点韵,或将诗行凑得略为整齐而显得不太散漫。后来则觉得原作既然有格律,译诗也应当有,于是尝试用我国传统诗形式,将诗译成齐言的或非齐言的长短句。但这对原作内容有较多改造,诗味也往往不同,感到译诗的形式最好还是取自原作。于是控制译诗行字数,使之与原作诗行的音节数相等或相应。这做法有直观效果,却未必合理,因为英语传统格律诗的诗行并不建立在音节上,而是建立在由轻重音节有规则排列而构成的节奏单位"音步"上,而现代汉语诗的节奏单位也不是"字"。后来得知译诗前辈卞之琳、屠岸先生"以顿代步"译法,认为合理,就让拙译"兼顾"诗行的顿数和字数,就是说,让译诗行的顿数、字数分别与原作行的音步数、音节数相等和相应,再加上韵式与原作韵式一致,译诗就反映了原作的三项基本格律要素:韵式、诗行顿数与字数。在迄今的英诗汉译中,这是反映原作格律形式最严格的要求。

读到了爱德华·菲茨杰拉德（Edward Fitzgerald, 1809—1883）的 The Rubáiyát of Omar Khayyám，其优美的文字和诗意让我深为所动。那严谨而较独特的格律，即使不谈格律是诗歌特具的文体特征，单看那格律从第一首到最后一首的贯彻始终，就让译者无法视而不见。我感到这正是练习译诗的绝佳材料，于是一首首译出又反复修改，让内容和格律形式逐步靠拢原作。后来这样的修改成了习惯，而我在这过程中越来越相信，译诗准确反映原作格律形式不仅可能，而且必要，因为除了审美意义，格律是诗歌音乐性保证，还蕴含文字中没有的信息，如诗的民族性、地域性、时代性、内容倾向以及作者诗歌观和创新意识等。

以菲茨杰拉德的 ruba'i（rubáiyát 为 ruba'i 的复数）而言，这种英诗的格律特点是韵式带东方色彩，第一、二、四行押尾韵（或四行都押），每行是 10 音节构成的 5 "音步"。这诗体出自中世纪中亚地区塔吉克和波斯一带的 roba'i，内容倾向于抒写人生哲理，菲氏于 19 世纪中引进并定型为一种英国诗体。

为尽可能准确反映这诗体的特色，拙译要求在准确反映原作内容的同时，也准确反映其格律形式，即韵式为 aaxa，每行译诗则固定为 12 字构成的 5 个节奏单位 "顿"，以反映原作行的 5 音步，"兼顾"了格律三要素。就这样，菲氏《柔巴依集》成为按此要求译出的第一本英诗。此后这要求用于其他拙译，成为拙译的明显特点，被称为 "三兼顾"。

这里要说明，为什么称 Rubáiyát 为《柔巴依集》，而不用郭沫若的译名《鲁拜集》。因为我发现维吾尔族有叫作 "柔巴依" 的传统诗，从发音和地域看，几乎可确定其与波斯 roba'i 的渊源关系。而为了反映"本是同根生"，自当用"柔巴依"，何况这发音更接近三音节的原文。我相信，郭沫若当初若知道维吾尔"柔巴依"，肯定会毫不犹豫地采用。而正因为他的译本是《鲁拜集》，尽管该书长期以来独步译界，读者只知道"鲁拜"是外国诗体，全然不知这是我国古已有之的"柔巴依"——可见，译名不当可能在认识上起阻断作用。

二

1981 年，拙译《柔巴依集》被上海译文出版社接受。翻译出版界前辈孙家晋先生建议我调入该社，我心头一热，没多考虑自己读大学时发现的眼疾，放弃了两年前通过考试得到的教职，开始当编辑，从此走定了译诗之路。《柔巴依集》中第 11 首作品，据称是 19 世纪引用最多的四行诗（见本书"第一部分"），下面按其句式道出这诗集与我的相逢和关系：

无花无果的院子里，一间陋屋；
昏黄灯光下，两本借来的旧书；
　从中，传来了远方诱人的歌声——
啊，柔巴依，你引我走出一条路。

受到《柔巴依集》的鼓励，又身处出版环境，而不少来稿需编辑加工才可出版，所有这些让我翻译热情高涨，"射门意识"大增，而且受到启发，要译新东西，避免没有自己特点的重译。事实上，在我退休前的十多年间，拙译很是"多样化"或杂乱化。除了译诗歌，还译了小说、寓言、散文，当然主要还是诗歌。

这期间的拙译包括三位英国诗人作品的最早汉译本：司各特的《末代行吟诗人之歌》，以及《华兹华斯抒情诗选》和《丁尼生诗选》——巧的是，这后两位和菲氏都是剑桥大学出身的名诗人。此外，我喜欢凭兴趣译诗，读到喜欢的原作就译，所以"散译"抒情诗不少并不断增多。于是先后编成六个集子：英汉对照与非英汉对照的英国诗、美国诗、爱情诗各一。

译小说主要在进出版社之后，因为来稿多为小说，我这方面锻炼很少，就译了些中篇和短篇。长篇只译过两部。先是在资料室看到高尔斯华绥（John Galsworthy, 1867–1933）的 *The Dark Flower*，实在喜欢就译了出来（这书的确好看，出版后即登上《文汇读书周报》(1991/1/19) 的"半月热门书排行榜"，在五本上榜书中位列第二）。另一部是英国小说和报刊文学之父笛福的代表作 *The Adventures of Robinson Crusoe*。这书原可不译，但坊间只见各种各样《鲁滨孙漂流记》，而鲁滨孙从无漂流经历，原作书名中也绝无"漂流"暗示，却莫名其妙在汉译中"被漂流"百年，为避免其继续"被漂流"下去，我只能像那个说皇帝没穿衣服的傻小子，把该书译为《鲁滨孙历险记》。

我在此期间开始发表有关译诗的拙文。可一提的是，《世界文学》和《中国翻译》于1990年先后发表文章，作者是两位名译家。他们的译诗方式不同，分别是控制诗行字数和"以顿代步"，所以各讲各的理，但都没注意到这两种译法可以"兼容"。当时《柔巴依集》问世已近10年,我按"兼顾"要求译各种格律诗约三万行,对这译法的合理可行已有充分把握,于是作为正式介绍,在《中国翻译》发表拙文《一种可行的译诗要求》——原来的标题是"一种新的译诗要求",因为当时我已发现,这种译诗要求在英诗汉译中前所未有,但不知为什么发表时"新"被改成了"可行"。

此文的发表有点故事性,发表后更引起我写此类文章的兴趣,随后写的拙文中,有几篇专门讨论诗的可译性,因为有些国内外权威断言诗不可译。我认为他们的说法过于绝对,而且语涉刻薄,就以他们自己的诗作或翻译为例反驳,说明他们的诗不可译论言过其实——迄今为止,尚未见到持诗不可译论者对拙文的反驳。

我感到,国内外诗不可译论的产生,很大程度上缘于一普遍现象,就是译诗忠实反映了原作内容,就较难忠实反映原作格律形式,反之亦然,就是说,译诗难以在忠实的基础上兼顾内容与形式的统一。这一点在拼音文字的译诗中尤其明显,但我根据实践发现,我们的汉语汉字具有独特的潜力,有可能处理好这样的兼顾或统一。

三

我1996年退休,至今的二十多年可分前后两段。前一段里主要出版了两部叙事诗和《英诗汉译学》。两部叙事诗是英诗之父乔叟(Geoffrey Chaucer, 1340?-1400)的代表作《坎特伯雷故事》(*The*

Canterbury Tales）和18世纪英国最著名诗人蒲柏（Alexander Pope, 1688–1744）的《秀发遭劫记》(*The Rape of the Lock*)。翻译那部中古英文巨著，对我来说，各方面都是极大挑战，为什么要译呢？

我退休前已视力残疾二级，不能再信马由缰译诗，应赶紧译更具标志性的作品了，而《坎特伯雷故事》是首选。该书在英国文学史上的地位不言而喻，而选择这书还有另一层考虑。因为拙译抒情诗虽说颇得好评，"兼顾"译法已在不同核心学刊上介绍，却很少译者采用。毕竟拙译拙文有限，在不反映原作格律几乎已成"传统"的英诗汉译中，不仅易被忽视或淹没，有时甚至被视为异类，认为拙译丧失了韵味，进入了"误区"，是"骗骗外行的"，等等——似乎译诗不反映原作格律形式是正道，更具原作韵味。我觉得译《坎特伯雷故事》既可彰显英诗格律传统，也凸显译诗反映原作格律的必要。因为这部英诗源头之作的主体虽然是诗，却也有散文，且两者分工不同；而诗也有分工不同的诗体，用于不同人物讲的故事。

选择《坎特伯雷故事》果然有效，只是显效的方式出我意外：出版后即获第四届全国优秀外国文学图书奖一等奖，而且，上下两册的平装本还是七个一等奖中得票最多的。

译这部书有个插曲。20世纪50年代中，我因多次发生严重意外，查出患有"眼科绝症"视网膜色素变性，当时视力还正常，只是视野大为缩小。到了退休时，视野已极度狭小，属视力残疾二级（一级为全盲），视力也大为减退。《坎特伯雷故事》译到一半，白内障已很严重，用放大镜看原作也不行了。但眼睛基础差，手术风险大，为避免翻译半途而废，熟悉我眼病的专家建议我尽可能晚动手术，每天用眼药水略微放大瞳孔，让进入眼内的光线多一点。就这样，我总算完成了《坎特伯雷故事》的翻译。

动手术前我还完成了译诗文集《从柔巴依到坎特伯雷——英语诗汉译研究》。这是我首个文集，或许也是有关英诗汉译的最早个人文集。此书属"翻译研究丛书"，再版时应出版社要求易名为《英语诗汉译研究——从柔巴依到坎特伯雷》。写到这里，我想到译诗前辈钱春绮先生，因为当时我颇有后顾之忧，怕半途而废，是钱先生鼓励我并答应我说，如果手术有意外，他将帮我读校样——后来虽无意外，钱先生的好意我至今铭记。

还要感谢现代科技和医术。我白内障手术虽有波折，仍"开发"出残存视力，延长了我的译龄。当然那以后我大为收敛，原有计划中只译了蒲柏的《秀发遭劫记》。此书篇幅远不到《坎特伯雷故事》十分之一，却让我感到必须停止翻译了。

白内障手术前，我已认识到，诗歌翻译和其他文学翻译的区别，主要在于诗歌是唯一有格律的文体，格律是诗歌的文体特征，是让语言美发挥到极致的有效手段，因此，译格律诗如果不反映原作格律，多半只是语意翻译而非诗歌翻译，有点像画孔雀而不着意描绘其羽毛。译诗现象看来纷繁杂乱，原因就在这里。然而看来的纷繁杂乱却有其内在的发展逻辑，因为这实际上是译诗方式演进的结果。下面就看各译诗方式出现的顺序。

开始时，译诗必然是我国传统诗形式，因为当时诗没有其他形式；但这样译诗容易失真，所以一出现自由的白话新诗，译诗就采用这样的语言和形式，以较准确地传达原作；不久，对反映原作内容有了把握,就开始注意反映原作形式,其中韵式的情况较简单,主要问题在于诗行。"等行翻译"容易做到,然后是讲究字数的译法,即译诗行字数与原作行字数相等或相应;接着,新诗人发现,白话诗的节奏单位不是字,而是多由二或三字构成的"顿"(或称"音组"等,也有一字顿和四字顿),于是有了讲究顿数与原作音步数一致的"以顿代步"译法;再进一步,就是结合了后两者的"三兼顾"译法。

基于这认识,我写了些文章,并记起申请编审职称时两位专家的评语:复旦大学的陆谷孙先生说到,我的译诗实践和论文已"开始形成体系";而本社的吴劳前辈也有这说法。我决定根据百多年我国的译诗实践,写一本《英诗汉译学》。该书于2007年出版,获中国大学出版社图书奖首届优秀学术著作奖一等奖——今年正好出增订版。

可以一提的是,《英诗汉译学》是我第一本用电脑做的书,因为书写痉挛使我写字费劲,笔迹不整,而且俯首写字也让颈椎不适,只得求助于我一直避免的电脑,但限于各方面条件,至今还不善使用。

四

退休后20多年的后一段,始于《英诗汉译学》出版之后。由于对英汉对照本的喜爱,我把三本非英汉对照的"散译"英美诗也做成英汉对照,同原先三个对照本一起,增删成九本。顺便说一句:"散译"的"效率"远低于译叙事诗,看一百首原作,最后译出的往往仅区区几首。而为了证明"三兼顾"译法普遍适用,寻找格律特殊作品的效率更低。

而且做这类诗集特别费时费力，当初没有复印机和电脑，每首原作还得多次打印并校对，成书却归在读物类，似乎不上档次。但我乐此不疲，凡有可能和有机会做成英汉对照的拙译，包括《秀发遭劫记》和《伊索寓言》都这样做了。至今，连本书在内，我已做了28种英汉对照译诗集——即使对眼力正常的译者来说，这大概也算是一项个人纪录了。

当然对照本也有用。首先，诗歌翻译容易变形走样，有原作对照就不只看到译者的"一面之词"，便于发现译文的问题，对译者也是督促。其次，译诗不反映原作格律的理由，往往说是这会影响内容的准确传达，但我不同意这说法，希望对照本中的拙译有助于说明：译诗有可能准确反映原作的内容和格律形式。再次，如今读者的英语水平普遍较高，也许有兴趣浏览原作或尝试译诗，对照本就提供了方便——对于专爱重译的编译者来说，这就更为方便，希望他们的重译在原译基础上有所提高。

做九个对照本时，偶尔也拾遗补缺译点诗，做完后仍放不下译诗，想到英语中的"滑稽诗"（comic verse），觉得可译这种诗"过瘾"，因为它们通常短小而有格律，译起来不费眼力。于是让女儿买了20来本，专看其中10行以下的，结果陆陆续续译了不少。

我本想以新编《柔巴依集》和《英文滑稽诗300首》作为译诗终点，却意外进入丰收期。原来，出版社对其他拙译也有兴趣，要了十多本。随后，我所有英汉对照译诗集被其他出版社要去，《英诗汉译学》也出增订版。这一来，除早先两本译诗文集，所有拙译拙著这次"倾巢而出"。这对我来说确实意外，尤其是，这些书中还有多本下节中提到的新译。

这段时间里，有关译诗的拙文似乎写得更多，因为我认识到，伟大诗歌的背后必然有完备格律体系的支撑，认识到译诗反映原作格律的必要，知道格律是格律诗的"身份代码"，凭其格律三要素，就可在庞大的格律体系中将其定位，看清其与其他诗在格律上的亲疏远近。任何民族的传统诗都有其格律体系，每首诗都是那体系的有机组成部分，即使自由诗，也只是格律诗的存在而显出其自由。所以，翻译格律诗理当反映原作的格律形式，不顾原作形式的翻译，抛弃的恰恰是诗歌特具的文体特征。

这一时期的拙文更倾向于报上发表，后来在《中华读书报》发了10篇长文，为的是让尽可能多的读者和编者了解译诗反映原作格律的必要和可能。我想，在促使译者提高译诗要求方面，这比发表在学刊上有效。因为翻译中也有"惰性"之类的东西，各种各样的"鲁拜"译本和鲁滨孙的不断"漂流"便是例子。

五

滑稽诗中最引人注意的作品是 limerick（我译为"立马锐克"），这种定型诗体原为打油诗专用，英国谐趣文学之父、画家利尔（Edward Lear, 1812—1888）以之写成的 *A Book of Nonsense*（胡调集）使这种诗大为普及，可谓到了妇孺皆知地步。

这诗体短小活泼，从其三长两短诗行的排印方式即可看出特色：诗的韵式为 aabba，第一、二、五行较长，押 a 韵；第三、四行较短，押 b 韵。我感到译这种诗轻松而有意义，可说明译诗有必要反映原作格律，因为其所以是诗,并非胡调内容,而是这内容符合诗律,如果只反映内容而不管格律,那么这语意翻译还有多少"意义"?用"立马锐克"来说,就是:

Limerick 是特制正宗格律诗,
Nonsense 的内容偏讲究形式,
　　因此,原作的诗形
　　翻译中若不作反映,
译诗中还剩下多少"意思"?

《胡调集》原作有两百多首,内容千奇百怪。拙译滑稽诗中只收了利尔等作者的少量作品,但开始让"立马锐克"定型,使之有原作的形式特点,也即韵式为 aabba,第一、二、五行较长,为十字(或音节)五顿,而第三、四行较短,为八字三顿。

想不到后来偶尔发现一本小书,让我回光返照般大译特译"立马锐克"。*Lyrics Pathetic & Humorous from A to Z* 是诗画集,作者杜拉克(Edmund Dulac,1882—1953)的图不但精美,24首"立马锐克"更是"升级版"[1]。我惊喜之下一气译出。随后又发现篇幅稍大的诗画集,那是插

---

[1] "升级版"表现在三方面:(1)这是按字母表顺序排列的系列诗,各字母都有以之开头的诗,各诗在诗集里位置固定,前后连续贯通,构成有机整体;(2)首行与末行的结尾词不再重复,这表明诗的内容有复杂化倾向;(3)各诗第一行结尾词及其修饰词的首字母与该诗起首字母一致,其他诗行中也多用这样的头韵(这特点在译文中以双声解决,但这在汉字中"看"不出来,不像原作中的头韵可一眼看出)。

图名家科瑞恩（Walter Crane，1845—1915）为林顿（W. J. Linton，1812—1897）作品配图的 *Baby's Own Aesop*，其中66首"宝宝的伊索"也很快译出。

这时我胆气大壮，觉得自己译过500多则伊索寓言，熟悉其内容，既然希腊散文寓言可译成英语诗，那么对英语散文寓言当然也可这样做，这不仅使汉译增添诗趣，而且别有意味。因为平时只见格律诗被译成自由诗或散文，反过来做岂不更有趣有味？于是译出《伊索寓言诗365首》(含"立马锐克"近600个)，然后一鼓作气译出利尔的《胡调集》。真是想不到，不得不告别翻译之际，limerick诗体竟让我大发少年狂，连译了多本"立马锐克"。[1]

这还不算。译完《胡调集》仍未尽兴，而且闲着又难受，于是想到伊索寓言中颇多一面之词，例如《牛和车轴》中，拉车的牛听得车轴吱吱嘎嘎响，就对车轴呵斥道："干什么乱哼乱叫！／拉这车，你出了多大力量？"读这寓言，我为承担全车重量的车轴感到不平，但当时这念头一闪而过，如今则可用"立马锐克"把此类想法记下，于是想到不花多少眼力做一本《伊索寓言诗365首》。当然这已不是翻译，是在眼病逼迫下的无奈转向，就像先前译滑稽诗和"立马锐克"那样。

待这本寓言完成，不算翻译而来的，我写出的"立马锐克"总数在1000以上，远超上面三本limerick原作总和，更超过拙译"柔巴依"，

---

[1] 但我译的顺序恰恰与原作出版先后相反。本书中，为反映limerick的发展，这些诗仍按原作出版的先后排列。显然，《伊索寓言诗365首》受《宝宝的伊索》启发才做，理当出版在后，然而，尽管按合同规定，《宝宝的伊索》应在2017年底前出版，但拙稿在责任编辑那里至今未见校样。这书本来或许可说是伊索寓言首个诗体汉译本，但"抢后"出版使其浪费了这个机会。

足以证明这汉语定型诗体方便实用。如今,"柔巴依"这定型诗体不仅存在于拙译,还受到我国一些诗人青睐,用于他们的写作并正式发表。"立马锐克"写起来更方便,连我都可以胡诌两首:

立马锐克被利尔做出名,
从此在英语世界大流行;
　画家科瑞恩、杜拉克
　给这种作品添颜色,
让英诗多一道特异风景。

伊索让动植物开腔说话,
利尔让他的诗专讲胡话;
　林顿用利尔的调子
　唱伊索的一些故事,
科瑞恩为师傅配上字画。

目前的英诗创作中,多见的是自由诗,这很自然。因为乔叟以来的600年里,各种音步格律诗争奇斗艳,无所不至,已得到充分发展,无数名篇佳作构成了英国人引以为自豪的诗歌大厦。反观我们的传统诗词,也同样证明伟大的诗歌殿堂需要完备的格律体系和丰富多彩的定型诗体。然而由于种种原因,我们的新诗虽然很早就有格律化尝试,但至今定型的,只有外来的十四行诗和俳句,多见的仍是自由诗。而看看英语格律诗的千姿百态,就可知道我们被抛荒的是怎样的诗歌沃野。好在诗歌是唯一有格律的文体,人们不会忘记这文体特征而不加以开发,因为格律上的创新也是诗人发挥想象力和创造力的领域。

在国外,诗歌翻译有一项重要使命,就是介绍和引进外国诗体,以丰富本国的品种。拙译准确反映了几百种不同格律的原作,《英诗汉译学》的下篇是"汉译英诗格律简谱",以三百多个例子构成一小小体系,既显示格律品种无限丰富的可能,也可供我国新诗的格律建设参考，因为构建诗歌大厦需要大梁大柱，也需要各式构件。

六

这集子里所有译诗的原作都是格律诗（包括惠特曼、庞德等的格律诗），没选小说，因为译小说既非我的主项，也未必说得出多少特点，而拙译的诗在准确反映原作格律形式上具有明显特色——关于这点，看看"鲁拜"和"柔巴依"，即可发现两者的不同；而如果看《鲁滨孙漂流记》和《鲁滨孙历险记》，译文的区别也许没那么明显。

根据我从开始到结束的翻译过程，集子里的选诗分四个部分："柔巴依"、英国诗、美国诗、"立马锐克"。选的几乎全是抒情诗，因为这比叙事诗更具特色，也可避免选诗片段化，让读者看到的都是完整作品——哪怕是短短两行。我觉得这比叙事诗片段更有可读性。

这四个部分大致可反映我的译诗历程：从定型诗"柔巴依"开始，到定型诗"立马锐克"结束，中间五花八门的诗则占据绝大部分篇幅。因为我希望本书有较多功能，读者通过它不仅能"微观"了解拙译英语诗，还能"宏观"了解英美诗概貌。所以这两部分可说是较有系统的两个小诗集，英美历朝历代名诗人大多在这里有亮相机会。我既爱好"散译"，就正好有条件这样做，但限于篇幅，每位诗人仅一首"配额"并倾向于较短作品，所以，格雷的《挽歌》和雪莱的《西风颂》等，虽为英语诗集必选，这里只能割爱。

当然，做这样的诗集要考虑很多方面，但对于眼力穷途末路的我，除了篇幅上的考虑，只能大致凭印象，在选诗上尽可能倾向于各方面的多样化。需要说明的是，本书首尾两部分的短诗数量不多，很快就能浏览一遍，且原作大多没有标题，所以目录中不一一列出。

* * *

我译英语诗的事，几年前已到尽头，编译诗的事如今也到尽头。回头望去，最大的遗憾就是常有匆忙感，未能从容反复打磨拙译，而自己各方面条件差，本当做得更仔细。特别是这个可作为自己"样本书"的最后一本，未能按习惯在出版前细读一遍并做些修改，[1]浪费了最后的改进机会。我相信，如今译者各方面条件比我好，如果重视对原作格律形式的反映，必定做得比我好，因为，用"立马锐克"来说就是：

文学殿堂里，诗歌是皇帝，
惟有他，穿得起格律外衣；
　译诗若扒光他衣裳，
　他同穷光蛋没两样——
说他是皇帝，谁会相信你？

虽然我对拙译有遗憾，但对选择译诗并无遗憾，我甚至感到，当

---

[1] 可顺便一提的是，拙译常被收进某些译诗集，但往往事先未同我联系（有的事后连样书也不寄，甚至还写错我名字），而我经常修改拙译，因此那些译诗多半是被我淘汰的旧译。更令人啼笑皆非的是，那些旧译被取用时还出错，甚至被编者任意改动。

初我偶遇英诗是我的幸运，因为译诗给了我很多欢愉时光（常常欢愉得忘了自己的眼疾），让我的后半生过得很充实，可以说，干任何其他行当都不会给我这样的充实感。这里，我仍然要以英美诗人的两行诗作结。请看美国诗人奥格登·纳什的"歪诗""Reminiscent Reflection"：

When I consider how my life is spent,
I hardly ever repent.

说它是"歪诗"，因为诗行参差的押韵对句在英诗中并非"正路"。那么为什么参差呢？因为正像我们打油诗专用诗体"三句半"中的末行，纳什也来这一手。英美读者熟悉弥尔顿名诗"On His Blindness"，见到纳什这诗，必然联想到弥尔顿该诗头两行：When I consider how my light is spent,/Ere half my days, in this dark world and wide...但纳什把第一行中的 light 换成发音相像的 life，出人意外地让第二行的内容和形式来个"急刹车"。如今，我不能将译诗"进行到底"，只得在此"刹车"，就借来弥尔顿的第一行，再借来纳什的第二行，凑成我的《回顾》：

When I consider how my light is spent,
I hardly ever repent.

最后，我要感谢老伴张人丽。她一直尽其所能，让我专心在翻译园地上耕作，这次更是全面帮困，除了选定篇目，其他的事大多是她一步一步摸索着帮我做的，可以说，没有她的帮助就没有我这最后一本书。我同样要感谢黄福海先生。他曾为拙著《英诗汉译学》先后两版做过不同索引，这次蒙他慨允为本书读校样，让我免除了后顾之忧。我相信，他认真细致的工作可确保本书的差错率减到最小。

本书书名"我得重下海去"，来自英国诗人梅斯菲尔德（1878—1967）名篇《恋海热》，正是在这首诗的强烈吸引下，我对英语诗产生了强烈的兴趣，并由此开始了约半个世纪的译诗。

黄杲炘

2020年5月

目/录

丛书编辑说明……………………………………………i

丛书总序………………………………罗选民 iii

译者自序………………………………黄杲炘 vii

第一部分
《欧玛尔·哈亚姆之柔巴依集》选……………3

第二部分
英国诗……………15

第三部分
美国诗……………189

第四部分
立马锐克……………351

黄杲炘译著年表……………**360**

PART ONE

From THE RUBÁIYÁT OF OMAR KHAYYÁM

第一部分

《欧玛尔·哈亚姆之柔巴依集》选

From THE RUBÁIYÁT OF OMAR KHAYYÁM[1]

I

Awake! for Morning in the Bowl of Night

Has flung the Stone that puts the Stars to Flight:

　　And Lo! the Hunter of the East has caught

The Sultán's Turret in a Noose of Light.

III

And, as the Cock crew, those who stood before

The Tavern shouted—"Open then the Door!

　　"You know how little while we have to stay,

"And, once departed, may return no more."

VII

Come, fill the Cup, and in the Fire of Spring

The Winter Garment of Repentance fling:

　　The Bird of Time has but a little way

To fly—and Lo! the Bird is on the Wing.

1　依据爱德华·菲茨杰拉德（Edward Fitz Gerald, 1809—1883）英译本第一段。

《欧玛尔·哈亚姆之柔巴依集》选

1

醒醒吧!黎明已在黑夜的碗中
投进那石球,叫星斗飞离天穹;
 看哪!那东方猎手的光明之索
已经把苏丹的塔楼稳稳套中。

3

公鸡开始啼叫;在酒肆的门外,
站着的人群喊道:"快把门打开!
 你知道,我们的逗留多么短暂,
而一旦离去,就永远不得回来。"

7

来,把杯盏斟满;往春天的火里
扔进你悔恨交加的隆冬外衣;
 时光之鸟只能飞短短的距离——
看哪!这只鸟不断在扑动双翼。

XI

Here with a Loaf of Bread beneath the Bough,

A Flask of Wine, a Book of Verse—and Thou

 Beside me singing in the Wilderness—

And Wilderness is Paradise enow.

XIV

The Worldly Hope men set their Hearts upon

Turns Ashes—or it prospers; and anon,

 Like Snow upon the Desert's dusty Face

Lighting a little Hour or two—is gone.

XIX

And this delightful Herb whose tender Green

Fledges the River's Lip on which we lean—

 Ah, lean upon it lightly! for who knows

From what once lovely Lip it springs unseen!

XXI

Lo! some we loved, the loveliest and best

That Time and Fate of all their Vintage prest,

 Have drunk their Cup a Round or two before,

And one by one crept silently to Rest.

11

这里,树荫下伴我的是个面包,
是一瓶葡萄美酒和一卷诗抄;
　　你也在我身旁,在荒漠中歌唱——
这个荒漠,够得上天堂般美好。

14

人们所心向神往的世俗企求
变成了灰烬或一团旺火;尔后,
　　像雪花飘落灰蒙蒙沙漠表面,
辉映了一时半刻便化为乌有。

19

草色喜人,毛羽般的新翠嫩绿
满江浒;在这里我们靠下身躯;
　　轻轻靠着吧!谁知道从前该是
多美的绛唇,才把它暗中化育!

21

瞧!我们钟爱的,是命运和时光
从其收获葡萄中榨出的琼浆——
　　他们已喝下各自的三杯两盏,
一个接一个悄悄爬进了睡乡。

XXIX

Into this Universe, and *why* not knowing,

Nor *whence*, like Water willy-nilly flowing:

   And out of it, as Wind along the Waste,

I know not *whither*, willy-nilly blowing.

XXXII

There was a Door to which I found no Key:

There was a Veil past which I could not see:

   Some little Talk awhile of ME and THEE

There seemed—and then no more of THEE and ME.

XXXVIII

One Moment in Annihilation's Waste,

One Moment, of the Well of Life to taste—

   The Stars are setting and the Caravan

Starts for the Dawn of Nothing—Oh, make haste!

XL

You know, my Friends, how long since in my House

For a new Marriage I did make Carouse:

   Divorced old barren Reason from my Bed,

And took the Daughter of the Vine to Spouse.

29

不知什么是缘由、哪里是源头，
就像是流水，无奈地流进宇宙；
　　不知哪里是尽头，也不再勾留，
我像是风儿，无奈地吹过沙丘。

32

门户紧锁，我没有找到它钥匙；
帷幕高张，我没法洞察和透视；
　　片言只语，**我**和**你**似乎被谈及——
而在这之后，**你**和**我**全将消逝。

38

寂灭的荒漠里作一片刻羁留；
片刻之中把生命之泉尝一口——
　　星斗沉落，瀚海中的旅行商队
向乌有之晨进发。快快喝个够！

40

你知道，朋友，为一次新的婚礼
我早就在家办过狂欢的酒席；
　　衰老不孕的理性被我赶下床，
娶来葡萄的女儿做我的爱妻。

XLVI

For in and out, above, about, below,

'Tis nothing but a Magic Shadow-show,

    Play'd in a Box whose Candle is the Sun,

Round which we Phantom Figures come and go.

LII

And that inverted Bowl we call The Sky,

Whereunder crawling coop't we live and die,

    Lift not thy hands to *It* for help—for It

Rolls impotently on as Thou or I.

LVII

Oh, Thou, who didst with Pitfall and with Gin

Beset the Road I was to wander in,

    Thou wilt not with Predestination round

Enmesh me, and impute my Fall to Sin?

LXVII

Ah, with the Grape my fading Life provide,

And wash my Body whence the Life has died,

    And in a Windingsheet of Vine-leaf wrapt,

So bury me by some sweet Garden-side.

46

进进又出出,上上下下地回迁——
这个只是一出走马灯的戏剧;
　灯里的蜡烛是太阳,在它周围
是我们这些幻影来来又去去。

52

那翻转的大碗我们唤作天空,
下面是我们生死其中的樊笼;
　别举起你双手求它给你帮助——
它转动之乏力也和你我相同。

57

你呀,你在我彷徨流浪的路上
布置下陷阱机关和美酒佳酿,
　该不会对我撒下命定的罗网,
再把堕落的罪名安在我头上?

67

请为我凋零的生命把酒置办,
请把我死去的身子洗涤一番,
　用葡萄的藤藤叶叶把我装裹,
埋我在某个美好的花园旁边。

LXXII

Alas, that Spring should vanish with the Rose!
That Youth's sweet-scented Manuscript should close!
   The Nightingale that in the Branches sang,
Ah, whence, and whither flown again, who knows!

LXXIII

Ah Love! could thou and I with Fate conspire
To grasp this sorry Scheme of Things entire,
   Would not we shatter it to bits—and then
Re-mould it nearer to the Heart's Desire!

LXXIV

Ah, Moon of my Delight who know'st no wane,
The Moon of Heav'n is rising once again:
   How oft hereafter rising shall she look
Through this same Garden after me—in vain!

72

唉,春天哪,竟随同玫瑰而消亡!
芬芳的青春手稿呀,也得合上!
　夜莺啊,曾在树枝间娇啼曼唱——
谁知它来自哪里又飞向何方!

73

爱人哪,你我若能同命运协力,
把握这全部事理的可悲设计,
　我们就不用先把它砸个粉碎,
再把它塑造得比较称心如意!

74

我的欢乐之月呀,你永不变细,
瞧那天边的月亮又一次升起:
　今后她将多少回照遍这园子
把我寻觅,但已见不到我踪迹!

PART TWO

British Poems

第二部分

英国诗

CONTENTS

GEOFFREY CHAUCER Griseld Is Dead

THOMAS WYATT 'Throughout the World, If It Were Sought'

HENRY HOWARD 'My Friend, the Things That to Attain'

QUEEN ELIZABETH I On Monsieur's Departure

EDMUND SPENSER Happy Ye Leaves

WALTER RALEIGH To His Son

PHILIP SIDNEY A Ditty

WILLIAM SHAKESPEARE Fidele

CHRISTOPHER MARLOWE The Passionate Shepherd to His Love

THOMAS CAMPION Cherry-Ripe

JOHN DONNE The Bait

BEN JONSON To Celia

ROBERT HERRICK Gather Ye Rosebuds

GEORGE HERBERT The Altar

JOHN MILTON To Mr. Cyriack Skinner upon His Blindness

RICHARD CRASHAW Not by Force (emblem)

JOHN DRYDEN Hidden Flame

JOHN WILMOT Impromptu on Charles II

COLLEY CIBBER The Blind Boy

ALEXANDER POPE Epitaph Intended for Sir Isaac Newton

THOMAS GRAY On a Favourite Cat, Drowned in a Tub of Goldfishes

目录

乔叟 (1340?—1400) 格里泽尔达已死亡

怀亚特 (1503—1542) "若有谁要把漂亮话寻找"

霍华德 (1517—1547) "朋友,要过上幸福的生活"

伊丽莎白一世 (1533—1603) 此君离别后

斯宾塞 (1552—1599) 幸福的书页

罗利 (1552?—1618) 示儿

锡德尼 (1554—1586) 短歌

莎士比亚 (1564—1616) 菲迪莉

马洛 (1564—1593) 多情的牧羊人致爱人

坎皮恩 (1567—1620) 熟啦,樱桃!

多恩 (1572—1631) 饵

琼森 (1573—1637) 致西莉亚

赫里克 (1591—1674) 快摘玫瑰蕾

赫伯特 (1593—1633) 祭坛

弥尔顿 (1608—1674) 同西里克·斯基纳先生谈失明

克拉肖 (1613?—1649) 不是靠蛮力(寓意诗)

德莱顿 (1631—1700) 暗藏的爱火

威尔莫特 (1647—1680) 即兴为查尔斯二世作

西勃 (1671—1757) 盲童

蒲柏 (1688—1744) 为牛顿爵士拟的墓铭

格雷 (1716—1771) 为溺死在金鱼缸中的爱猫而作

WILLIAM BLAKE Auguries of Innocence

ROBERT BURNS 'O My Luve Is Like a Red, Red Rose'

WILLIAM WORDSWORTH The Lost Love

WALTER SCOTT Lochinvar

SAMUEL TAYLOR COLERIDGE The Sad Story

ROBERT SOUTHEY The Scholar

WALTER SAVAGE LANDOR On His Seventy-Fifth Birthday

THOMAS MOORE The Light of Other Days

ALLAN CUNNINGHAM 'A Wet Sheet and a Flowing Sea'

GEORGE GORDON BYRON She Walks in Beauty

PERCY BYSSHE SHELLEY A Lament

JOHN KEATS The Human Seasons

HARTLEY COLERIDGE Early Death

ELIZABETH BROWNING Inclusion

CAROLINE E. S. NORTON I Do Not Love Thee

ALFRED TENNYSON Crossing the Bar

ROBERT BROWNING Meeting at Night

EMILY BRONTË The Old Stoic

ARTHUR HUGH CLOUGH 'Say Not, the Struggle Naught Availeth'

DANTE GABRIEL ROSSETTI Three Shadows

CHRISTINA ROSSETTI A Birthday

布莱克 (1757—1827) 天真之兆

彭斯 (1759—1796) "啊，我爱人像红红的玫瑰"

华兹华斯 (1770—1850) 失去的爱

司各特 (1771—1832) 洛钦瓦

S. T. 柯尔律治 (1772—1834) 伤感的故事

骚塞 (1774—1843) 学者

兰多 (1775—1864) 为七十五岁生日而作

T. 穆尔 (1779—1852) 往日的光辉

坎宁安 (1784—1842) "湿淋淋的帆索，滚滚的海"

拜伦 (1788—1824) 走动着的她是一片美艳

雪莱 (1792—1822) 哀歌

济慈 (1795—1821) 人的四季

H. 柯尔律治 (1796—1849) 早逝

伊丽莎白·勃朗宁[1] (1806—1861) 包容

诺顿夫人 (1808—1877) 我并不爱你

丁尼生 (1809—1892) 过沙洲，见领航

R. 勃朗宁 (1812—1889) 夜会

艾米莉·勃朗特 (1818—1848) 坚忍澹泊的长者

克拉夫 (1819—1861) "不要说斗争没什么用处"

D. G. 罗塞蒂 (1828—1882) 三重影

克里斯蒂娜·罗塞蒂 (1830—1894) 生日

---

[1] 本书中为便于识别，女诗人译名一概用全名，男诗人只用姓氏，若有相同姓氏，则姓氏前用名字首字母。

WILLIAM MORRIS Love Is Enough

ALGERNON CHARLES SWINBURNE 'Love Laid His Sleepless Head'

AUSTIN DOBSON In After Days

THOMAS HARDY 'Ah, Are You Digging on My Grave'

ROBERT BRIDGES 'When First We Meet We Did Not Guess'

WILLIAM ERNEST HENLEY Invictus

ROBERT LOUIS STEVENSON Requiem

OSCAR WILDE In the Gold Room (A Harmony)

ALFRED EDWARD HOUSMAN Loveliest of Trees

MARY COLERIDGE Slowly

WILLIAM BUTLER YEATS 'Down by the Salley Gardens'

RUDYARD KIPLING Coward

ERNEST DOWSON Cynara

WILLIAM HENRY DAVIES Leisure

RALPH HODGSON Stupidity Street

WALTER DE LA MARE Silver

JOHN MASEFIELD Sea-Fever

JOSEPH CAMPBELL The Old Woman

JAMES STEPHENS The Snare

JAMES JOYCE 'O Sweetheart, Hear You'

DAVID HERBERT LAWRENCE Green

EDWIN MUIR The Castle

THOMAS STEARNS ELIOT Cat Morgan Introduces Himself

W. 莫里斯 (1834—1896) 爱就已足够

斯温伯恩 (1837—1909) "没法睡着觉的爱神"

多布森 (1840—1921) 在身后的日子里

哈代 (1840—1928) "哦,你这是在刨我的坟土"

布里吉斯 (1844—1930) "我们初见时哪能料到"

亨利 (1849—1903) 不屈不挠

斯蒂文森 (1850—1894) 挽歌

王尔德 (1854—1900) 在金色房间里 (一段和声)

豪斯曼 (1859—1936) 最可爱的树

玛丽·柯尔律治 (1861—1907) 意迟迟

叶芝 (1865—1939) "在那些杨柳园子边"

吉卜林 (1865—1936) 胆小鬼

道森 (1867—1900) 希娜拉

戴维斯 (1871—1940) 闲暇

霍奇森 (1871—1962) 愚蠢街

德拉梅尔 (1873—1956) 银

梅斯菲尔德 (1878—1967) 恋海热

J. 坎贝尔 (1879—1944) 老妇

斯蒂芬斯 (1882—1950) 机关

乔伊斯 (1882—1941) "心上人,听听你"

劳伦斯 (1885—1930) 绿

缪尔 (1887—1959) 城堡

艾略特 (1888—1965) 摩根猫的自我介绍

HUGH MACDIARMID The Storm-Cock's Song

ROBERT GRAVES The Face in the Mirror

ROY CAMPBELL Autumn

CECIL DAY-LEWIS Song: 'Come, Live with Me and Be My Love'

LOUIS MACNEICE Christina

STEPHEN SPENDER Word

DYLAN THOMAS 'Do Not Go Gentle into That Good Night'

PHILIP LARKIN Talking in Bed

THOM GUNN Considering the Snail

ROGER MCGOUGH 40—Love

SEAMUS HEANEY The Forge

麦克迪尔米德 (1892—1978) 大鸫之歌

格雷夫斯 (1895—1985) 镜中的脸

R. 坎贝尔 (1901—1957) 秋

戴－刘易斯 (1904—1972) 歌："来与我同住，做我的爱人"

麦克尼斯 (1907—1963) 克莉斯蒂娜

斯彭德 (1909—1995) 字眼

托马斯 (1914—1953) "不要温顺地进入那美好晚上"

拉金 (1922—1985) 在床上谈话

冈恩 (1929—2004) 细看蜗牛

麦克高夫 (1937—) 40：0

希尼 (1939—2013) 打铁铺

GEOFFREY CHAUCER

Griseld Is Dead[1]

Griseld is dead, and eke her patience,

And both alike are buried, cold and pale;

And hence I cry, in open audience,

No wedded man should boldly thus assail

His spouse's patience, in the hope to find

Griselda's; for he certainly will fail.

O noble wives, well blessed with providence,

Bid no humility your tongue to nail;

Let never clerk have cause or diligence

To write of you so marvelous a tale

As of Griselda, patient, mild and kind,

Lest 'Lean Cow' swallow you in her entrail![2]

---

1 这是英诗之父乔叟代表作《坎特伯雷故事》中"牛津学士的故事"的"跋"。故事讲的是意大利民女嫁给贵族，受到种种匪夷所思的"考验"而逆来顺受，终于感动丈夫，结果皆大欢喜。乔叟在这里反对丈夫这做法，号召女性为捍卫自己的尊严和权利而斗争。这在600多年前十分难得，同样难得的是其格律：36行等长的诗行构成六个诗节，诗节的韵式均为ababcb，且用韵一样，也即a韵出现12次，b韵出现18次，c韵出现6次，这在韵部较窄的英语中有很大难度，故被称为"乔叟的押韵奇迹"。原作为中古英语，这里用的是乔叟专家Walter William Skeat的现代英语译文，其文字与乔叟原作略有差异，但格律上符合原作。

2 Lean Cow是法国古老寓言中的怪物，只吃为数极少的坚忍妇女，所以极瘦。相反，双角怪兽以食为数众多的坚忍男人为生，所以极肥。

乔叟 (1340?—1400)

格里泽尔达已死亡

格里泽尔达同她的那种耐心
都已经苍白冰凉,早就被埋葬;
为此我要向世人公开喊一声:
结婚的男人绝不该如此狂妄,
为把格里泽尔达的耐心寻觅
而刁难妻子,因为他准会失望。

高贵的妻子,你们天生很聪明,
别让谦卑把你们的舌头锁上,
别让文人有那份理由或热心,
像写格里泽尔达的耐心一样,
写你们温顺仁爱的非凡事迹,
免得被瘦牛吞进了它的胃肠!

Like Echo, keep no silent diffidence,[1]

But, always answering back, be prompt to rail;

Be ne'er deluded by your innocence,[2]

But sharply let your tyranny prevail.

Imprint full well this lesson in your mind,

For profit, such as may your hearts regale.

Ye arch-wives, stand upon your own defence,

Since ye are strong as is a mighty whale;

Nor suffer men to do the least offence.

And slender wives, that in the fight are frail,

Be eager as a tiger is in Ind,

And clatter like a mill-wheel or a flail.

Ne'er stand in dread, nor show them reverence;

For though thy husband should be armed in mail,

The arrows of thy bitter eloquence

Shall through his breast or helmet work him bale;

In jealousy endeavour him to bind,

And thou shalt make him cower as doth a quail.

1　Echo 音译为厄科，是希腊神话中的女山神，因爱情遭拒而憔悴，最后只剩下声音。

2　英语诗歌中，为符合诗律，常省略音节，这里的 ne'er 是 never 之略。

要像回声女神，别怕得不出声，
要敏捷地作出反应，责骂对方；
千万别因为纯真就受到欺蒙，
要抢上风把你们的厉害张扬；
这条教训要牢牢记在脑海里，
好处是，这能让你们的心欢畅。

机警强悍的妻子，要捍卫自身；
既然你们像鲸鱼那样地强壮，
男人的欺侮一点也不要容忍；
瘦弱的妻子，要像印度虎那样
灵活又勇猛，千万别不堪一击；
要像磨坊的水车轮格格作响。

别怕他们，对他们别毕恭毕敬；
哪怕你丈夫把甲胄穿在身上，
用你那言词之箭的尖利锋刃
透过他胸甲和头盔把他刺伤；
努力用妒忌把他捆住，我劝你，
他就会畏畏缩缩像鹌鹑一样。

If thou be fair, be well in evidence;

Display thy visage, and thy garments trail;

If ugly, spare not to incur expense,

And get thee friends by bidding men 'all hail!'

Be light of mien as linden-leaves in wind,

And let him weep, and wring his hands, and wail!

THOMAS WYATT

'Throughout the World, If It Were Sought'

Throughout the world, if it were sought,

    Fair words enough a man shall find:

They be good cheap, they cost right nought,

    Their substance is but only wind:

But well to say and so to mean,

That sweet accord is seldom seen.

如果你很俊,就让人家看看清;
向大家展示你的容貌和着装;
如果你很丑,那就要争取友情,
见了人就要问好,花钱得豪爽;
神情轻松得就像风中的树叶——
让丈夫扭绞双手流着泪哭嚷!

怀亚特 (1503—1542)

"若有谁要把漂亮话寻找"

若有谁要把漂亮话寻找,
　　会发现世上满是这东西;
这东西便宜得分文不要,
　　因为究其实只是一口气;
话说得好听又真心实意,
很少见这样美好的统一。

HENRY HOWARD

'My Friend, the Things That to Attain'

My friend, the things that to attain
   The happy life be these, I find:
The riches left, not got with pain;
   The fruitful ground; the quiet mind;

The equal friend; no grudge, no strife;
   No charge of rule, nor governance;
Without disease, the healthy life;
   The household of continuance;

The mean diet, no dainty fare;
   Wisdom joined with simpleness;
The night dischargéd of all care,
   Where wine the wit may not oppress;

The faithful wife, without debate;
   Such sleeps as may beguile the night;
Content thyself with thine estate,
   Neither wish death, nor fear his might.

霍华德 (1517—1547)

"朋友,要过上幸福的生活"

朋友,要过上幸福的生活,
　　我发现少不了这样几条:
有家传财产,不用去干活;
　　心情既宁静,土地又丰饶;

有同样亲友,不怨也不争;
　　不受拘管,也不需治天下;
无病无灾,过日子讲卫生;
　　家庭里,继承者并不缺乏;

吃粗菜淡饭而不吃佳肴;
　　要有简朴中包含的明智;
到夜里也没有任何烦恼,
　　也不会让酒侵扰了神思。

还有不争长论短的贤妻,
　　加上一夜到天亮的安睡;
你对自己的景况挺满意,
　　不想死也不怕死神逞威。

QUEEN ELIZABETH I

On Monsieur's Departure

I grieve and dare not show my discontent,
    I love and yet am forced to seem to hate,
I do, yet dare not say I ever meant,
    I seem stark mute but inwardly do prate.
I am and not, I freeze and yet am burned,
Since from myself another self I turned.

My care is like my shadow in the sun,
    Follows me flying, flies when pursue it,
Stands and lies by me, doth what I have done.
    His too familiar care doth make me rue it.
No means I find to rid him from my breast,
Till by the end of things it be suppressed.

Some gentler passion slide into my mind,
    For I am soft and made of melting snow;
Or be more cruel, love, and so be kind.
    Let me or float or sink, be high or low.
Or let me live with some more sweet content,
Or die and so forget what love are meant.

伊丽莎白一世 (1533—1603)

此君离别后

我伤心,但是不敢让难过流露;
　我在爱,却被迫装出我是在恨;
我做事,可不敢说出我的意图;
　我心中嘀咕,表面却一声不吭。
我是是否否,冰凉却像着了火;
因为,我已变成了另一个自我。

我的心事,像我阳光下的黑影,
　我逃它就跟着我,我追它就逃;
时时跟随我,做我做过的事情。
　对他的魂牵梦萦使得我懊恼,
但没法在自己的心中排除他,
除非万事都了结这才能压下。

请把温和的激情送进我脑海;
　爱神哪,因为我像融雪般地柔;
要不就对我更狠,这也是仁爱。
　让我不是高就是低,或沉或浮。
让我活,就多给些满足的甜蜜;
让我死,我就能忘掉爱的含义。

EDMUND SPENSER

Happy Ye Leaves[1]

Happy ye leaves! whenas those lily hands,
    Which hold my life in their dead-doing might,
Shall handle you, and hold in love's soft bands,
    Like captives trembling at the victor's sight.
    And happy lines! on which with starry light,
Those lamping eyes will deign sometime to look,
    And read the sorrows of my dying sprite,
Written with tears in heart's close bleeding book.
And happy rhymes! bathed in the sacred brook
    Of *Helicon*, whence she derived is;[2]
When ye behold that angel's blessed look,
    My soul's long lacked food, my heaven's bliss;
        Leaves, lines, and rhymes, seek her to please alone,
        Whom if ye please, I care for other none![3]

---

1 本诗出自文艺复兴时期的著名十四行诗组诗 *Amoretti*（小爱神），该组诗含 88 首，这是第一首。诗中对象后来是作者妻子。

2 Helicon 一译赫利孔，是希腊神话中文艺女神缪斯们居住的山名，山边有两股泉水，据传是诗歌和诗灵感的源泉。

3 十四行诗出自意大利，由怀亚特和霍华德引进英国。其结构常分上下两片，前八行韵式 abba abba，后六行韵式略有变化，但最后两行互不押韵。英国十四行诗的结构则有变化，这也反映在韵式上，如这里的斯宾塞体十四行诗，韵式为 abab bcbc cdcd ee（排列上可清楚显示韵式）。

斯宾塞 (1552—1599)

幸福的书页

幸福的书页！那双百合般的手
  以其致命的威力操着我生命；
你们被那手爱怜翻动的时候，
  像俘虏在胜利者面前抖不停。
  幸福的诗行！那双明灯般眼睛
有时候还会赏光看一看你们，
  读我奄奄待毙灵魂中的哀情——
这是泣血的心写下的书一本。
幸福的韵！她出自圣泉赫利肯
  而你们有幸沐浴在这圣泉中；
我灵魂就缺这粮，而至高福分
  是你们将会看到她那种仙容；
    书页、诗行和韵哪，去讨她喜欢！
    倘博得她欢心，旁的我全不管。

WALTER RALEIGH

To His Son

Three things there be that prosper up apace

And flourish, whilest they grow asunder far,

But on a day they meet all in one place,

And when they meet, they one another mar;

And they be these, the wood, the weed, the wag.[1]

The wood is that which makes the gallow tree,

The weed is that which strings the hangman's bag,

The wag, my pretty knave, betokeneth thee.

Mark well, dear boy, whilest these assemble not,

Green springs the tree, hemp grows, the wag is wild,

But when they meet, it makes the timber rot,

It frets the halter, and it chokes the child.

    Then bless thee, and beware, and let us pray

    We part not with thee at this meeting day.[2]

1 　这里有意用三个首字母相同的词（头韵）。一般来说，这在译文中很难反映。
2 　这首作品不像其他早期十四行诗用于写爱情。本诗采用英国式韵式 abab cdcd efef gg，也称莎士比亚体。

罗利 (1552？—1618)

示儿

有三样东西如果分开着生长,
总是生长得又快又好又出色,
但要是有一天凑在一个地方,
它们彼此间就会相残又相剋;
三样东西是木头、麻和美少年。
有了木头,就可以把绞架竖起;
有了麻,就有刽子手那种项圈;
而那美少年,孩子,就是代表你。
听好了:只要这三者不在一道,
树就绿,麻就长,少年生龙活虎;
而三者一旦碰上,木头就烂掉,
绞索就磨损,少年就一命呜呼。
　所以要注意,得求上天保佑你,
　让我们别在那一天同你分离。

PHILIP SIDNEY

A Ditty

My true-love hath my heart, and I have his,
    By just exchange one for another given:
I hold his dear, and mine he cannot miss,
    There never was a better bargain driven:
        My true-love hath my heart, and I have his.

His heart in me keeps him and me in one,
    My heart in him his thoughts and senses guides:
He loves my heart, for once it was his own,
    I cherish his because in me it bides:
        My true-love hath my heart, and I have his.

WILLIAM SHAKESPEARE

Fidele[1]

Fear no more the heat o' the sun[2]
    Nor the furious winter's rages;
Thou thy worldly task hast done,

---

1 本诗为《辛白林》中的歌谣,菲迪莉是伊莫琴女扮男装时的假名。
2 o' = of,但这里为的是在诗律上可不计这个音节。下面 ta'en = taken 也一样。

锡德尼 (1554—1586)

短歌

我的心给了爱人,他的心给了我;
　我们是公平地交换,把心儿对调:
他的心我当宝,我的心他也藏妥;
　比这更好的交易,永远也找不到。
　　我的心给了爱人,他的心给了我。
他的心,在我的胸中合我俩为一;
　我的,在他胸中引导感觉和思想;
他爱我的心,因为那曾经是他的;
　我怜他的心,因为在我这个胸膛。
　　我的心给了爱人,他的心给了我。

莎士比亚 (1564—1616)

菲迪莉

别再怕太阳晒得火辣辣,
　别再怕狂暴冬风呼呼吹;
干完人间事你就回老家,

Home art gone and ta'en thy wages:
Golden lads and girls all must,
As chimney-sweepers, come to dust.

Fear no more the frown o' the great,
　Thou art past the tyrant's stroke;
Care no more to clothe and eat;
　To thee the reed is as the oak:
The scepter, learning, physic, must
All follow this, and come to dust.

Fear no more the lightning-flash
　Nor the all-dreaded thunder-stone;
Fear not slander, censure rash;
　Thou hast finish'd joy and moan:
All lovers young, all lovers must
Consign to thee, and come to dust.

你已把你的报酬全领回:
金童玉女都得走这条路——
就像扫烟囱小孩归尘土。

别再怕大人物眉头蹙紧,
　暴君的打击你已无所谓;
别再为衣食操劳又担心,
　对于你,橡树无异于芦苇:
管什么帝王、学者或大夫,
大家得走这条路归尘土。

别再怕天上的飞火闪电,
　别再怕个个都怕的雷轰;
别再怕人家的碎语闲言,
　你已不再有欢乐和悲痛:
年轻恋人都得走这条路,
都像你一样也得归尘土。

CHRISTOPHER MARLOWE

The Passionate Shepherd to His Love[1]

Come live with me and be my love,
And we will all the pleasures prove
That hills and valleys, dale and field,
And all the craggy mountains yield.

There will we sit upon the rocks
And see the shepherds feed their flocks,
By shallow rivers, to whose falls
Melodious birds sing madrigals.

There will I make thee beds of roses
And a thousand fragrant posies,
A cap of flowers, and a kirtle
Embroidered all with leaves of myrtle.

---

1 Marlowe 的同时代人 Raleigh、Donne(见后)及后代诗人对此诗都有反应,他们的诗多以本诗头一行开始,大多采用本诗格律。

马洛（1564—1593）

多情的牧羊人致爱人

来与我同住，做我的爱人，
这里的田野、嶙峋的山峰
和幽谷间的所有开心事，
我们全都要一一去证实。

我们要一起坐在岩石上，
看那些牧人把羊群放养；
伴着潺潺流的清浅小河，
啼声宛转的鸟雀唱着歌。

我要为你做玫瑰的床铺，
为你做千百个芬芳花束，
还要给你做长裙和花冠——
裙子上绣满桃金娘叶瓣。

A gown made of the finest wool,

Which from our pretty lambs we pull,

Fair lined slippers for the cold,

With buckles of the purest gold.

A belt of straw and ivy buds

With coral clasps and amber studs:

And if these pleasures may thee move,

Come live with me and be my love.

The shepherd swains shall dance and sing

For thy delight each May-morning:

If these delights thy mind may move,

Then live with me and be my love.

THOMAS CAMPION

Cherry-Ripe[1]

There is a garden in her face

---

1 cherry-ripe 是当时叫卖樱桃的用语。

用我们漂亮羊羔的毫毛
给你做精纺细织的长袍;
还做舒服的软鞋御寒气——
有纯金搭扣,有洁白衬里。

腰带用麦秆和藤芽编成——
珊瑚做搭扣,琥珀为饰钉:
这些开心事若让你动心,
就来同我住,做我的爱人。

为让你喜欢,五月的早上
年轻牧羊人跳舞又歌唱;
这些欢乐若打动你的心,
就来同我住,做我的爱人。

坎皮恩 (1567—1620)

熟啦,樱桃!

她的脸蛋上有一座花园,

Where roses and white lilies grow;
 A heavenly paradise is that place,
Wherein all pleasant fruits do flow;
  There cherries grow which none may buy,
  Till 'Cherry-Ripe' themselves do cry.

 These cherries fairly do enclose
Of orient pearl a double row,
 Which when her lovely laughter shows,
They look like rose-buds fill'd with snow:
  Yet them nor peer nor prince can buy,
  Till 'Cherry-Ripe' themselves do cry.

 Her eyes like angels watch them still;
Her brows like bended bows do stand,
 Threat'ning with piercing frowns to kill
All that attempt with eye or hand
  Those sacred cherries to come nigh,
  —Till 'Cherry-Ripe' themselves do cry!

长着玫瑰和洁白的百合；
　那里是一座天堂般乐园，
里面有种种美味的鲜果；
　　那里的樱桃谁也买不到，
　　　除非它自己叫："熟啦，樱桃！"

　那美好的樱桃团团围住
晶莹光洁的好珍珠两行，
　她嫣然一笑，珍珠就显露——
像玫瑰花蕾含着雪一样：
　　这樱桃，王公贵人买不到，
　　　除非它自己叫："熟啦，樱桃！"

　她双眼像守樱桃的天使，
她眉毛像挽开着的硬弓；
　对这些圣洁的樱桃，要是
谁敢用眼光或手去靠拢，
　　那蹙眉像要把谁射杀掉，
　　　直到它自己叫："熟啦，樱桃！"

JOHN DONNE

The Bait

Come live with me and be my love,
And we will some new pleasures prove,
Of golden sands and crystal brooks,
With silken lines and silver hooks.

There will the river whispering run,
Warmed by thine eyes more than the sun.
And there the enamoured fish will stay,
Begging themselves they may betray.

When thou wilt swim in that live bath,
Each fish, which every channel hath,
Will amorously to thee swim,
Gladder to catch thee, than thou him.

If thou, to be so seen, beest loath,
By sun or moon, thou darkenest both;
And if myself have leave to see,
I need not their light, having thee.

多恩 (1572—1631)

饵

来与我同住,做我的爱人,
来体验从未经历的欢欣:
金色沙滩边,朝清澈溪流
放下丝线扎住的小银钩。

那潺潺溪流感到的温暖
来自你眼波,与阳光无关。
着迷的鱼儿在那里逗留,
为了让自己上钩而恳求。

你若要在那活水中沐浴,
大江小河里各种各样鱼
都会情意绵绵地游向你,
它抓你,比你抓它更乐意。

若不愿这样被日月看见,
你就使日光月光都暗淡;
而如果你能允许我欣赏,
有了你,我无须它们的光。

Let others freeze with angling reeds,

And cut their legs with shells and weeds,

Or treacherously poor fish beset

With strangling snare or windowy net.

Let coarse bold hands from slimy nest

The bedded fish in banks out-wrest,

Or curious traitors, sleave-silk flies,

Bewitch poor fishes' wandering eyes.

For thee, thou needest no such deceit,,

For thou thyself art thine own bait;

That fish that is not catched thereby,

Alas, is wiser far than I.

BEN JONSON

To Celia[1]

Drink to me only with thine eyes,
 And I will pledge with mine;

1　本诗这种八行节的韵式较特殊，为 abcbabcb。

让别人提着钓竿不挪窝，
腿脚被野草和贝壳扎破；
或者为可怜的鱼布置好
阴险的网和要命的圈套。

让鲁莽的手把歇着的鱼
从泥泞的洞里猛地攫取，
让精致的假蝇这种奸细
把游移可怜的鱼眼蒙蔽。

而你呢，不用玩这种把戏，
因为，鱼饵也就是你自己！
唉，一条鱼能不被你钓到，
那么，它远远比我要乖巧。

琼森 (1573—1637)

致西莉亚

只要你用眼神为我干杯，
　我也用我的来祝酒；

Or leave a kiss but in the cup
　　And I'll not look for wine.
The thirst that from the soul doth rise
　　Doth ask a drink divine;
But might I of Jove's nectar sup,
　　I would not change for thine.

I sent thee late a rosy wreath,
　　Not so much honouring thee
As giving it a hope that there
　　It could not wither'd be;
But thou thereon didst only breathe
　　And sent'st it back to me;
Since when it grows, and smells, I swear,
　　Not of itself but thee!

要不，你单在杯中留个吻，
　　我也便不再觅香酎。
我灵魂深处只渴望一醉，
　　把神妙的琼浆企求；
然而即使有仙酒给我饮，
　　我不愿把你的换走。

我新近送你一束玫瑰花，
　　与其说向你表敬意，
不如说希望它在你身旁
　　有可能永久开下去；
可你只对花呼吸了几下，
　　就把它送回我这里；
真的，它从此散发的馨香
　　不属于它而属于你！

ROBERT HERRICK

Gather Ye Rosebuds

Gather ye rosebuds while ye may,
    Old Time is still a-flying;
And this same flower that smiles to-day,
    To-morrow will be dying.

The glorious Lamp of Heaven, the Sun,
    The higher he's a-getting
The sooner will his race be run,
    And nearer he's to setting.

That age is best which is the first,
    When youth and blood are warmer,
But being spent, the worse, and worst
    Times, still succeed the former.

Then be not coy, but use your time;
    And while ye may, go marry:
For having lost but once your prime,
    You may for ever tarry.

赫里克 (1591—1674)

快摘玫瑰蕾

快摘玫瑰蕾，趁你还年少，
　　时光在飞逝个不停；
今朝这朵花还含着微笑，
　　到明天它就会凋零。

太阳，这光辉灿烂的天灯，
　　越是快升到天中心，
就越是接近跑完它全程，
　　离落山也就越是近。

最早的年轻时代最惬意，
　　那时候血热青春富；
但以后接踵而来的时期
　　就一个比一个不如。

所以别忸怩，要把握时机，
　　要趁你年轻就成婚；
因为你一旦任韶光逝去，
　　就可能会蹉跎一生。

GEORGE HERBERT

The Altar[1]

A broken ALTAR, Lord, thy servant rears,
Made of a heart, and cemented with tears:
Whose parts are as thy hand did frame:
No workman's tool hath touched the same.
      A   Heart   alone
      Is   such a stone ,
      As   nothing   but
      Thy power doth cut .
      Wherefore each part
      Of my hard heart
      Meets in this frame ,
      To praise thy Name :
That, if I chance to hold my peace ,
These stones to praise thee may not cease .
Oh let thy blessed SACRIFICE be mine ,
And sanctify this ALTAR to be thine .

1　本诗是 pattern poems（象形诗）代表作，也正由于本诗，这种诗也称"圣坛诗"。这些诗能排成一定的形式有其格律根据（同时也利用英语词与词之间的空隔调节）。这类诗的特点可说就在于形式。从译文可看出，"兼顾顿数与字数"译法的合理与必要。

赫伯特 (1593—1633)

祭坛

主啊一个破**祭坛**是您的忠仆
用一颗心筑起又用泪水粘固:
  它各个部分像由您建造,
  匠人的工具哪里能碰到。
    也只有一颗**心**
    才石头般坚硬,
    除了您没有谁
    有力量叫它碎。
    所以我这硬心
    凭它的各部分
    合成了这形状,
    把您的**名**颂扬:
  这样,若我有幸得安宁,
  这些石块将不停颂扬您。
但愿哪我有做您**牺牲**的福分,
愿您接纳这**祭坛**而使之神圣。

JOHN MILTON

To Mr. Cyriack Skinner upon His Blindness

Cyriack, this three years' day these eyes, though clear

    To outward view of blemish or of spot,

    Bereft of light their seeing have forgot;

Nor to their idle orbs doth sight appear

Of sun or moon or star throughout the year,

    Or man or woman. Yet I argue not

    Against Heaven's hand or will, nor bate a jot

Of heart or hope, but still bear up and steer

Right onward. What supports me, dost thou ask?

    The conscience, friend, to have lost them overplied

In liberty's defense, my noble task,

    Of which all Europe talks from side to side.

This thought might lead me through the world's vain mask

    Content, though blind, had I no better guide.[1]

---

1 Milton 有 23 首十四行诗。他用的意大利韵式，但是内容一气呵成，没有上八下六之分。

弥尔顿 (1608—1674)

同西里克·斯基纳先生谈失明

西里克，三年来尽管我这双眼
　　看来无斑无瑕，却丧失了目光——
　　一无用处的眼珠把视觉遗忘；
太阳、月亮和星星都整年不见，
男子、妇女的身影也不再出现。
　　我不埋怨上天的意志和巨掌，
　　不让信心和希望受丝毫影响，
始终坚忍而坚定地勇往直前。
也许你要问：我靠什么来支持？
　　靠良知，朋友；我为了捍卫自由
累坏了双眼，而我这崇高职责，
　　人们口口相传，已传遍了全欧。
若没有更好向导，我凭这认识
　　可眼暗心安把人间假面看透。

RICHARD CRASHAW

Not by Force (emblem)[1]

'Tis not the work of force but skill

To find the way into man's will.

'Tis love alone can hearts unlock.

Who knows the Word, he needs not knock.

JOHN DRYDEN

Hidden Flame

I feed a flame within, which so torments me

That it both pains my heart, and yet contents me:

'Tis such a pleasing smart, and I so love it,

That I had rather die than once remove it.

Yet he, for whom I grieve, shall never know it;

---

[1] 这种"寓意诗"流行于文艺复兴晚期的欧洲,通常由三部分组成:图、格言和说明这两者关系的诗。图的意义往往隐晦,诗则指出与格言一致的寓意。本诗是"寓意诗"佳作,起点虽也是意义并不明朗的图,却比一般"寓意诗"进一步:那颗心右面有"铰链",表明这心可以打开,只是被左面一个卷轴般东西"锁"住了,这东西上的文字意为"秘诀",也即只有知道秘诀,才可把心打开。

克拉肖 (1613?—1649)

不是靠蛮力 (寓意诗)

不是靠蛮力而是凭技巧,
能找到进人心思的通道。
只有爱能把心头锁开启。
谁知道秘诀,叩门就不必。

德莱顿 (1631—1700)

暗藏的爱火

我心中烧的一团火把我折磨,
它使我快活又使我心里难过:
这种使人高兴的痛苦我喜爱,
宁可死也不愿让这痛苦离开。

但让我伤心的他可不能知道;

My tongue does not betray, nor my eyes show it.

Not a sigh, nor a tear, my pain discloses,

But they fall silently, like dew on roses.

Thus, to prevent my Love from being cruel,

My heart's the sacrifice, as 'tis the fuel;

And while I suffer this to give him quiet,

My faith rewards my love, though he deny it.

On his eyes will I gaze, and there delight me;

While I conceal my love no frown can fright me.

To be more happy I dare not aspire,

Nor can I fall more low, mounting no higher.

JOHN WILMOT

Impromptu on Charles II[1]

Here lies a great and mighty king

 Whose promise none relies on;

---

[1] 查尔斯二世即英王查理二世 (1630—1685)。他早年生活平淡,其父查理一世被处决后,他被立为苏格兰国王,后流亡法国。克伦威尔死后,他被迎回英国,1661 年在威斯敏斯特大教堂加冕为英格兰与爱尔兰国王,但命运多舛,常遭议会和臣民强烈不满。这首诗虽墓铭形式,但他并未去世,而且还作出了答复。

我的嘴和眼得把这秘密守牢。
我不让叹息和眼泪暴露痛苦,
叹息和流泪,轻得像花上降露。

这样,为不让心上人变得心狠,
我作为燃料的心就成了牺牲;
我承受这磨难,为了给他安宁,
我自有补报,虽然他没还我情。

我爱细看他眼睛,看了真舒服;
我不流露爱,他皱眉我不在乎。
对于更大的幸福,我不敢希望:
不攀高,就不会跌到更低地方。

威尔莫特 (1647—1680)

即兴为查尔斯二世作

这里躺着的国王很强大,
　　但没人信他的诺言;

He never said a foolish thing,

    Nor ever did a wise one.

COLLEY CIBBER

The Blind Boy

O say what is that thing call'd Light,

    Which I must ne'er enjoy;

What are the blessings of the sight,

    O tell your poor blind boy!

You talk of wondrous things you see,

    You say the sun shines bright;

I feel him warm, but how can he

    Or make it day or night?

My day or night myself I make

    Whene'er I sleep or play;

And could I ever keep awake

    With me 'twere always day.

他向来都不说一句傻话,

　　聪明事也没做一件。

西勃 (1671—1757)

盲童

哦,唤作光的是什么东西?——

　　偏偏我永远难享用!

有眼力是什么样的福气?

　　请告诉可怜的盲童。

你说你看到奇妙的东西,

　　说太阳辉煌又灿烂;

我能感觉到他温暖,但是

　　怎造成白天和夜晚?

我的白天和夜晚我知道——

　　凭我在睡觉还在玩;

我要是能够永远不睡觉,

　　就一直生活在白天。

With heavy sighs I often hear

    You mourn my hapless woe;

But sure with patience I can bear

    A loss I ne'er can know.

Then let not what I cannot have

    My cheer of mind destroy:

Whilst thus I sing, I am a king,

    Although a poor blind boy.

ALEXANDER POPE

Epitaph Intended for Sir Isaac Newton

Nature and Nature's laws lay hid in night:

God said, *Let Newton be!* and all was light.[1]

1　作者为强调牛顿贡献之大，套用了《旧约全书·创世记》1章3节句式：God said, Let there be light: and there was light（中文《圣经》为：上帝说要有光，就有了光）。

我常听见你深深的叹息——
　　为我的不幸而悲切；
但我准能够忍受这损失——
　　因为我对它不了解。

所以，别让得不到的东西
　　来坏了我的好心情；
我这样唱着，像国王得意——
　　虽说是可怜的盲童。

蒲柏 (1688—1744)

为牛顿爵士拟的墓铭

自然和自然法则，在黑夜中隐藏。
上帝说要有牛顿！就全都有了光。

THOMAS GRAY

On a Favourite Cat, Drowned in a Tub of Goldfishes[1]

'Twas on a lofty vase's side,

Where China's gayest art had dyed

   The azure flowers that blow,

Demurest of the tabby kind,

The pensive Selima, reclined,

   Gazed on the lake below.

Her conscious tail her joy declared:

The fair round face, the snowy beard,

   The velvet of her paws,

Her coat that with the tortoise vies,

Her ears of jet, and emerald eyes,

   She saw; and purr'd applause.

Still had she gazed, but 'midst the tide

Two angel forms were seen to glide,

   The Genii of the stream:

---

1 本诗以"尾韵诗节"（tail-rhyme stanza）写成，这种法国诗体很早引进英国，常用于传奇（如乔叟《坎特伯雷故事》中的"托帕斯爵士"），也称"传奇六行节"（romance-six）。

格雷 (1716—1771)

为溺死在金鱼缸中的爱猫而作

一个高高鱼缸的瓷壁上，
画着的几朵蓝花正开放——
　　中国的釉彩真华美；
沉思的塞丽玛趴在缸沿，
那一派端庄是雌猫典范：
　　她凝视着下面湖水。

通灵性的尾巴流露欣喜：
漂亮的圆脸，雪白的髭须，
　　掌心肉同鹅绒一样，
她的外衣同玳瑁能比美，
双耳若黑玉，两眼如翡翠；
　　她边看边呜呜夸奖。

她一动不动地凝望，只见
涟漪里有两位水中神仙
　　天使般地戏波逐浪：

Their scaly armour's Tyrian hue[1]
Through richest purple to the view
    Betray'd a golden gleam.

The hapless Nymph with wonder saw:
A whisker first, and then a claw,
    With many an ardent wish
She stretch'd, in vain, to reach the prize—
What female heart can gold despise?
    What Cat's averse to Fish?

Presumptuous maid! with looks intent
Again she stretch'd, again she bent,
    Nor knew the gulf between—
Malignant Fate sat by and smiled—
The slippery verge her feet beguiled;
    She tumbled headlong in!

Eight times emerging from the flood
She mew'd to every watery God

---

1 Tyre 为黎巴嫩西南部港市,古代为腓尼基奴隶制城邦,《圣经》中称推罗。推罗紫是当地以多种海贝制的染料,价格昂贵,在希腊、罗马时代,这颜色织物象征权力和财富。

鳞片的颜色都是推罗紫——
那两副甲胄色彩既富丽,
　　还隐隐闪出了金光。

不幸的佳丽看得犯了傻:
先凑上髭须,又伸出脚爪,
　　但撩不到那对宝贝,
尽管她伸呀捞呀使足劲——
妇道家怎么能鄙薄黄金?
　　鱼怎会叫猫咪腻味?

冒失的小姐!她目光专注,
一次又一次弯腰又伸足,
　　不知道跟前是深渊,
而厄运之神坐在边上笑——
溜滑的缸沿耍了她的脚:
　　她一头栽到水里面!

她八次冒出这一片汪洋,
喵喵喵呼叫河仙与海王,

Some speedy aid to send:—
No Dolphin came, no Nereid stirr'd,[1]
Nor cruel Tom nor Susan heard—
　　A favourite has no friend!

From hence, ye Beauties, undeceived,
Know one false step is ne'er retrieved,
　　And be with caution bold:
Not all that tempts your wandering eyes
And heedless hearts, is lawful prize,
　　Nor all that glisters, gold![2]

WILLIAM BLAKE

Auguries of Innocence

To see a world in a grain of sand
And a Heaven in a wild flower,
Hold Infinity in the palm of your hand
And Eternity in an hour.

1　据传说，海豚会把落水的人驮到岸边（"伊索寓言"中有此类故事）。Nereid 为海中骑海马等海兽的女仙；下一行中的 Tom 和 Susan 是男女仆人名。
2　见英谚 All that glitters is not gold。

求他们快点来搭救；
但海豚和水神都没出现，
凶汤姆和苏珊也没听见——
　　得宠者哪里有朋友！

美人哪，但愿你们能醒悟；
要知道，失足恨永难弥补；
　　所以要大胆要细心：
引你们眼迷神乱的东西
不全是你们的合法奖励——
　　闪光的不全是黄金！

布莱克 (1757–1827)

天真之兆

从一颗沙子把世界看清，
从野花把天堂感悟，
用一时半刻把永恒包孕，
用手掌把无穷握住。

ROBERT BURNS

'O My Luve Is Like a Red, Red Rose'

O my Luve is like a red, red rose,
  That's newly sprung in June:
O my Luve is like the melodie,
  That's sweetly played in tune.

As fair art thou, my bonie lass,
  So deep in luve am I;
And I will luve thee still, my dear,
  Till a' the seas gang dry.

Till a' the seas gang dry, my dear,
  And the rocks melt wi' the sun;
And I will luve thee still, my dear,
  While the sands o' life shall run.

And fare-thee-weel, my only Luve!
  And fare-thee-weel a while!
And I will come again, my Luve,
  Tho' it were ten thousand mile.

彭斯 (1759—1796)

"啊,我爱人像红红的玫瑰"

啊,我爱人像红红的玫瑰
  在六月里刚刚开放;
啊,我爱人像甜美的旋律
  演奏得和谐又酣畅。

你那样漂亮,我的好姑娘,
  我爱你也就那样深;
我将永远爱着你,亲爱的,
  直爱到四海水枯尽。

爱到四海水枯尽,亲爱的,
  爱到山晒得都化掉;
我将永远爱着你,亲爱的,
  只要我的心还在跳。

再见吧,我唯一心爱的人!
  容我们暂时地分离!
但我一定要回来,心上人,
  哪怕是相隔三万里。

WILLIAM WORDSWORTH

The Lost Love[1]

She dwelt among the untrodden ways
    Beside the springs of Dove,
A Maid whom there were none to praise
    And very few to love:

A violet by a mossy stone
    Half hidden from the eye!
—Fair as a star, when only one
    Is shining in the sky.

She lived unknown, and few could know
    When Lucy ceased to be;
But she is in her grave, and, oh,
    The difference to me!

1　本诗可称华兹华斯的代表作,属于"露西组诗"。标题为后人所加。这种诗节在英诗中常见,称"圣歌诗节"或"谣曲诗节"。

华兹华斯 (1770—1850)

失去的爱

她住在人迹罕到的路边,
　　住在野鸽泉的近旁;
这姑娘生前没有人称赞,
　　也很少人把她爱上。

一朵半遮半掩的紫罗兰,
　　开在长青苔的石旁!
美好得像颗星孤孤单单,
　　闪闪地在天上放光。

活着时谁知道她在人间,
　　更有谁知道她夭亡;
但露西已在坟墓里长眠,
　　对我呀人间变了样!

WALTER SCOTT

Lochinvar

O, young Lochinvar is come out of the west,
Through all the wide Border his steed was the best,[1]
And save his good broadsword he weapons had none;
He rode all unarmed, and he rode all alone.
So faithful in love, and so dauntless in war,
There never was knight like the young Lochinvar.

He stayed not for brake, and he stopped not for stone,
He swam the Eske river where ford there was none;
But, ere he alighted at Netherby gate,
The bride had consented, the gallant came late:
For a laggard in love, and a dastard in war,
Was to wed the fair Allen of brave Lochinvar.

So boldly he entered the Netherby hall,
Among bride's-men and kinsmen, and brothers and all;
Then spoke the bride's father, his hand on his sword
(For the poor craven bridegroom said never a word),

1　the Border 指苏格兰和英格兰的交界地区。

司各特 (1771—1832)

洛钦瓦

年轻的洛钦瓦从西部赶来——
广袤的边区里他的马最快；
大砍刀就是他全部的武器，
没戴盔没穿甲他独自奔驰。
论爱得忠诚，论敢斗敢拼杀，
没哪个骑士比得上洛钦瓦。

灌木丛和石头滩挡他不住，
没涉水的浅滩就下河泅渡；
但在奈泽比堡门口下马前，
姑娘许了人：他来得已太晚。
一个懦夫和爱情上的傻瓜
正要做新郎，不是他洛钦瓦。

他昂首阔步进城堡的厅堂——
那全是主人家亲友和傧相；
可怜的新郎害怕得不吭声，
新娘的父亲手按着剑把问：

'O come ye in peace here, or come ye in war,

Or to dance at our bridal, young Lord Lochinvar?'

'I long wooed your daughter, my suit you denied; —

Love swells like the Solway, but ebbs like its tide —

And now I am come, with this lost love of mine,

To lead but one measure, drink one cup of wine.

There are maidens in Scotland more lovely by far,

That would gladly be bride to the young Lochinvar.'

The bride kissed the goblet; the knight took it up,

He quaffed off the wine, and he threw down the cup,

She looked down to blush, and she looked up to sigh,

With a smile on her lips and tear in her eye.

He took her soft hand, ere her mother could bar, —

'Now tread we a measure!' said young Lochinvar.

So stately his form, and so lovely her face,

That never a hall such a galliard did grace;

While her mother did fret, and her father did fume,

And the bridegroom stood dangling his bonnet and plume;

And the bride-maidens whispered, ''Twere better by far

To have matched our fair cousin with young Lochinvar.'

"你来这婚礼是要和是要打,
还是来跳跳舞,爵爷洛钦瓦?"

"我早求过婚,你已回绝我——
爱情像潮水,会涨也会落——
我爱情落空,这次来只求
跳上一次舞,喝一杯喜酒。
苏格兰还有更可爱的娇娃,
很乐意嫁给年轻的洛钦瓦!"

新娘吻了吻酒杯,他拿过来
一饮而尽后把杯子就一摔;
新娘羞红了脸又抬头叹息,
嘴边挂微笑,眼角是泪滴。
他握住新娘手,说"我们跳吧!"
新娘妈来不及挡住洛钦瓦。

他相貌堂堂,新娘也娇美,
舞会上哪有这样的好一对!
新娘的父母又焦躁又气恼,
而新郎呆立着弄帽上羽毛;
那些女傧相都低声在说话:
"美丽的表姐该嫁给洛钦瓦。"

One touch to her hand, and one word in her ear,

When they reached the hall door, and the charger stood near;

So light to the croupe the fair lady he swung,

So light to the saddle before her he sprung!

'She is won! we are gone, over bank, bush, and scaur;

They'll have fleet steeds that follow,' quoth young Lochinvar.

There was mounting 'mong Graemes of the Netherby clan;

Forsters, Fenwicks, and Misgraves, they rode and they ran;

There was racing, and chasing, on Canobie Lee,

But the lost bride of Netherby ne'er did they see.

So daring in love, and so dauntless in war,

Have ye e'er heard of gallant like young Lochinvar?

SAMUEL TAYLOR COLERIDGE

The Sad Story

To meet, to know, to love, and then to part,

Is the sad tale of many a human heart.

他舞到拴马的厅堂大门口,
一捏舞伴手,耳边说声"走",
将小姐轻轻往马鞍后一放,
自己也一纵身跳到马鞍上!
"得手啦!这就去跋山涉水吧!
他们的快马难追我洛钦瓦。"

奈泽比家的人纷纷上马背,
好几家亲友也帮着一起追;
他们跑遍又找遍了坎诺比,
但没见到被抢新娘的踪迹。
论爱得忠诚,论敢斗干拼杀,
有谁比得上豪侠的洛钦瓦?

S. T. 柯尔律治 (1772—1834)

伤感的故事

相逢、相知、相爱,然后相别离——
这伤感的故事,留在多少人心里。

ROBERT SOUTHEY

The Scholar

My days among the Dead are past;
    Around me I behold,
Where'er these casual eyes are cast
    The mighty minds of old;
My never-failing friends are they,
With whom I converse day by day.

With them I take delight in weal
    And seek relief in woe;
And while I understand and feel
    How much to them I owe,
My cheeks have often been bedew'd
With tears of thoughtful gratitude.

My thoughts are with the Dead; with them
    I live in long-past years,
Their virtues love, their faults condemn,
    Partake their hopes and fears,
And from their lessons seek and find
Instruction with an humble mind.

骚塞 (1774—1843)

学者

每天我都和古人在一起；
　　我随意地四下浏览，
无论我眼光落到了哪里，
　　总看见古代的圣贤：
他们是永远忠贞的朋友，
每一天都同我谈话交流。

我总爱找他们分享愉快，
　　忧伤时就去找慰藉；
只要我感觉到并且明白
　　受他们多少的教益，
从思想深处萌发的感激
常让我脸上挂下了泪滴。

我同古人生活在很久前，
　　思想也与之在一起，
爱他们德行，批他们缺点，
　　分担其希望和恐惧，
我从它们的经验教训里
虚心地汲取指点和教益。

My hopes are with the Dead; anon
    My place with them will be,
And I with them shall travel on
    Through all Futurity;
Yet leaving here a name, I trust,
That will not perish in the dust.

WALTER SAVAGE LANDOR

On His Seventy-Fifth Birthday

I strove with none, for none was worth my strife,
    Nature I loved and, next to Nature, Art;
I warmed both hands before the fire of life;
    It sinks, and I am ready to depart.

THOMAS MOORE

The Light of Other Days

Oft in the stilly night,
    Ere slumber's chain has bound me,
Fond memory brings the light

在古人那里我寄托希望；
　　不久后我们将一起，
会一起继续漂泊和游荡，
　　把整个的未来经历；
但我相信，我留下的名字
不会在这儿尘土中销蚀。

兰多 (1775—1864)

为七十五岁生日而作

我与世无争，因为我不屑同谁争：
　　大自然我热爱，其次，艺术也喜爱。
生活的火上，我把手烘得热腾腾；
　　火现在快熄灭，我已准备好离开。

T. 穆尔 (1779—1852)

往日的光辉

常常，在寂静的夜里，
　　当睡眠还没锁住我，
总会有多情的回忆

Of other days around me:

    The smiles, the tears

    Of boyhood's years,

The words of love then spoken;

    The eyes that shone,

    Now dimm'd and gone,

The cheerful hearts now broken!

Thus, in the stilly night,

    Ere slumber's chain has bound me,

Sad memory brings the light

    Of other days around me.

When I remember all

    The friends so link'd together

I've seen around me fall

Like leaves in wintry weather,

    I feel like one

    Who treads alone

Some banquet-hall deserted,

    Whose lights are fled,

    Whose garlands dead,

And all but he departed!

Thus in the stilly night

用往日光辉笼住我:
　　那青春年岁——
　　那些笑与泪,
　那充满了爱的话语;
　　但炯炯的眼
　　已变得暗淡,
　但欢乐的心已碎去!
这样,在寂静的夜里,
　当睡眠还没锁住我,
总会有伤感的回忆
　用往日光辉笼住我。

一个又一个紧相连,
　我想起所有的亲友;
他们像树叶在冬天,
眼看着零落在四周。
　像宴会结束
　　宾客都离去,
大厅里变得空落落;
　　华灯已熄灭
　　花环已凋谢,
　还在留连的只有我!
这样,在寂静在夜里,

Ere slumber's chain has bound me,

Sad Memory brings the light

Of other days around me.

ALLAN CUNNINGHAM

'A Wet Sheet and a Flowing Sea'

A wet sheet and a flowing sea,
 A wind that follows fast
And fills the white and rustling sail
 And bends the gallant mast;
And bends the gallant mast, my boys,
 While like the eagle free
Away the good ship flies, and leaves
 Old England on the lee.

O for a soft and gentle wind!
 I heard a fair one cry;
But give to me the snoring breeze
 And white waves heaving high;
And white waves heaving high, my lads,
 The good ship tight and free—

当睡眠还没锁住我,
总会有伤感的回忆
　　用往日光辉笼住我。

坎宁安 (1784—1842)

"湿淋淋的帆索,滚滚的海"

湿淋淋的帆索,滚滚的海,
　　飞快的风儿在追赶;
它鼓满沙沙作响的白帆,
　　它吹弯挺拔的桅杆;
吹弯挺拔的桅杆,男儿们!
　　这好船鹰一样飞翔,
正在飞离古老的英格兰,
　　留她在我们的后方。

但愿哪,来一阵轻柔和风!——
　　我听过美人的呼唤;
但我要呼呼劲吹的海风,
　　要奔涌的白浪滔天;
奔涌的白浪滔天,伙伴们!
　　这好船严实又奔放——

The world of waters is our home,
    And merry men are we.

There's tempest in yon hornéd moon,
    And lightning in yon cloud;
But hark the music, mariners!
    The wind is piping loud;
The wind is piping loud, my boys,
    The lightning flashes free—
While the hollow oak our palace is,
    Our heritage the sea.

GEORGE GORDON BYRON

She Walks in Beauty

She walks in beauty, like the night
    Of cloudless climes and starry skies;[1]
And all that's best of dark and bright
    Meet in her aspect and her eyes:
Thus mellowed to that tender light
    Which heaven to gaudy day denies.

---

1 本诗歌颂威尔莫特·霍顿夫人,她当时的丧服上饰有闪闪发亮的金属小片,故云。

我们的家是这水的世界,
　　我们哪是多么欢畅。

那边的半月预示着风暴,
　　那边的云间闪电光;
可水手们哪,听听这音乐!
　　风儿的歌声多嘹亮;
它的歌声多嘹亮,男儿们!
　　雷电的忽闪多爽朗——
橡木造的船是我们宫殿,
　　我们的封地是海洋。

拜伦 (1788—1824)

走动着的她是一片美艳

走动着的她是一片美艳,
　　就像是无云的夜晚星空;
明和暗的所有绝妙优点
　　汇聚在她的容貌和眼中:
就这样融合成柔润光线,
　　浓艳的白天没这份恩宠。

One shade the more, one ray the less,
    Had half impair'd the nameless grace
Which waves in every raven tress,
    Or softly lightens o'er her face,
Where thoughts serenely sweet express
    How pure, how dear their dwelling-place.[1]

And on that cheek and o'er that brow
    So soft, so calm, yet eloquent,
The smiles that win, the tints that glow
    But tell of days in goodness spent,
A mind at peace with all below,
    A heart whose love is innocent.

PERCY BYSSHE SHELLEY

A Lament

O World, O Life, O Time!

On whose last steps I climb,

    Trembling at that where I had stood before;

1　"思想"的"住所"即人的头颅。

增一分暗影或减一分光,
　　会使那无名之美受损害;
这种美波动在她乌发上,
　　柔和地辉映着她的两腮;
流露在脸上的娴静思想,
　　表明其住所的纯洁可爱。

她整个面容雅致而恬静,
　　但是那意态胜过多少话;
迷人的微笑,焕发的红晕,
　　表明了只同善有缘的她——
心思与天下的一切无争,
　　而心中的爱也高洁无瑕。

雪莱 (1792—1822)

哀歌

哦世界!哦人生!哦岁月!
我登上那最后的台阶,
　　颤抖着回顾我曾登临的所在;

When will return the glory of your prime?
    No more — Oh, never more!

Out of the day and night
A joy has taken flight:
    Fresh spring, and summer, and winter hoar
Move my faint heart with grief, but with delight
    No more — Oh, never more!

JOHN KEATS

The Human Seasons

Four seasons fill the measure of the year;
    There are four seasons in the mind of Man:
He has his lusty Spring, when fancy clear
    Takes in all beauty with an easy span:
He has his Summer, when luxuriously
    Spring's honey'd cud of youthful thought he loves
To ruminate, and by such dreaming high
    Is nearest unto heaven: quiet coves
His soul has in its Autumn, when his wings
    He furleth close; contented so to look

你峥嵘往日的荣光何时续接?
　　哦,不再——永不再!

无论是白天是黑夜,
那欢情已匆匆离别:
　　任凭是春是夏是冬日雪皑皑,
都叫我疲惫的心伤悲,而欢悦——
　　哦,不再——永不再!

济慈 (1795—1821)

人的四季

四个季节把一年的时间填满,
　　人的心灵也同样含四个季节:
他有朝气蓬勃的春天,一瞬间,
　　清晰的俊赏收进了美的一切;
在他的夏季,他爱把年轻思想
　　春天里采集的花蜜反复寻味,
细细品尝那蜜汁的甘甜芳香,
　　乘着那高远的冥想冲天而飞;
他心灵之秋有着小湾般安谧,
　　这时他心满意足地收拢翅膀,

On mists in idleness—to let fair things
　　Pass by unheeded as a threshold brook:
He has his Winter too of pale misfeature,
Or else he would forego his mortal nature.

HARTLEY COLERIDGE[1]

Early Death

She pass'd away like morning dew
　　Before the sun was high;
So brief her time, she scarcely knew
　　The meaning of a sigh.

As round the rose its soft perfume,
　　Sweet love around her floated;
Admired she grew—while mortal doom
　　Crept on, unfear'd, unnoted.

Love was her guardian Angel here,
　　But Love to Death resign'd her;

---

[1] 这位诗人是前面 S. T. Coleridge 的长子。

闲看着雾色；赏心悦目的万事
　像小河淌过门前，不在他心上；
他也有面目全非的苍白冬天，
除非他走在自然的逝去之前。

H. 柯尔律治 (1796—1849)

早逝

她的消逝像早晨的露滴，
　太阳还没有升得高；
她倏忽而过，叹息的意义
　她几乎都还不知道。

玫瑰的周围浮动着清香，
　她四周也洋溢着爱；
她长得令人爱慕，但死亡
　不为她所知地掩来。

爱神是她这里的保护神，
　却把她托死神照料；

Tho' Love was kind, why should we fear
But holy Death is kinder?

ELIZABETH BROWNING

Inclusion

Oh, wilt thou have my hand, Dear, to lie along in thine?
As a little stone in a running stream, it seems to lie and pine.
Now drop the poor pale hand, Dear, unfit to plight with thine.

Oh, wilt thou have my cheek, Dear, drawn closer to thine own?
My cheek is white, my cheek is worn, by many a tear run down.
Now leave a little space, Dear, lest it should wet thine own.

Oh, must thou have my soul, Dear, commingled with thy soul?—
Red grows the cheek, and warm the hand; the part is in the whole:
Nor hands nor cheeks keep separate, when soul is joined to Soul.

爱神已够好,我们还担心
　神圣的死神不更好?

伊丽莎白·勃朗宁 (1806—1861)

包容

啊,亲爱的,你真的要让我的手放进你的手?
像溪流中的小石头,看上去躺在那儿很难受。
不配同你的手一起立誓,请放下这可怜的手。

啊,亲爱的,你真的要让我脸颊贴近你脸颊?
我脸颊苍白又憔悴,因为很多泪曾沿它淌下。
亲爱的,挪开一点吧,免得泪水沾湿你脸颊。

啊,亲爱的,你非要我心灵同你的合而为一?
我的脸颊泛红,手变暖;部分已归入了整体。
当心灵与心灵相结合,手和脸颊就不会分离。

CAROLINE E. S. NORTON

I Do Not Love Thee

  I do not love thee!—no! I do not love thee!
And yet when thou art absent I am sad;
  And envy even the bright blue sky above thee,
Whose quiet stars may see thee and be glad.

  I do not love thee!—yet, I know not why,
Whate'er thou dost seems still well done, to me:
  And often in my solitude I sigh
That those I do love are not more like thee!

  I do not love thee!—yet, when thou art gone,
I hate the sound (though those who speak be dear)
  Which breaks the lingering echo of the tone
Thy voice of music leaves upon my ear.

  I do not love thee!—yet thy speaking eyes,
With their deep, bright, and most expressive blue,
  Between me and the midnight heaven arise,
Oftener than any eyes I ever knew.

诺顿夫人 (1808—1877)

我并不爱你

　　我并不爱你！对，我并不爱你！
可你不在的时候我感到忧伤，
　　还把你头上晴朗的蓝天妒忌，
因为星星默默看着你会欢畅。

　　我并不爱你！但不知什么道理，
你做的一切看来总尽美尽善；
　　孤寂独处的时候我频频叹息：
我爱的人同你比相差那么远！

　　我并不爱你！但在你离开之后，
你音乐般的话音总留在耳边；
　　我不管是哪个亲近的人开口，
总怨他把这缭绕的余音打断。

　　我并不爱你！可你那深邃明亮、
表情丰富得像说话的蓝眼睛，
　　总是在夜半浮现在我的上方；
别的眼睛从没出现得这样勤。

I know I do not love thee! yet, alas!

Others will scarcely trust my candid heart;

And oft I catch them smiling as they pass,

Because they see me gazing where thou art.

ALFRED TENNYSON

Crossing the Bar[1]

Sunset and evening star,

 And one clear call for me!

And may there be no moaning of the bar,

 When I put out to sea,

But such a tide as moving seems asleep,

 Too full for sound and foam,

When that which drew from out the boundless deep

 Turns again home.

Twilight and evening bell,

 And after that the dark!

---

[1] 本诗被认为是以死亡为主题的诗歌中最美的一首。这并不是丁尼生的最后作品，但他要求将本诗置于他一切作品集之末。

我知道我不爱你！可是天知道！
我这坦率心里话人家却怀疑；
　　我发觉他们走过时总带微笑，
因为他们看见我眼睛盯着你。

丁尼生 (1809—1892)

过沙洲，见领航

　　夕阳坠，晚星出，
一个呼声唤我多清楚！
　　　当我出海去，
　　河口沙洲莫悲哭。

　　海深邃，洋空阔，
潮来深海总须回头流；
　　　满潮水悠悠，
　　流水似睡静无皱。

　　暮色降，晚钟起，
钟声之后便是幽幽夜！

And may there be no sadness of farewell,

    When I embark;

For though from out our bourne of Time and Place

    The flood may bear me far,

I hope to see my Pilot face to face

    When I have crossed the bar.

ROBERT BROWNING

Meeting at Night

The grey sea and the long black land;

And the yellow half-moon large and low;

And the startled little waves that leap

In fiery ringlets from their sleep,

As I gain the cove with pushing prow,

And quench its speed i' the slushy sand.[1]

Then a mile of warm sea-scented beach;

Three fields to cross till a farm appears;

1　i' = in，但不计音节。本诗诗节韵式较特殊，为 abccba。

当我登船去，
　别离时分莫哽咽。

　　人间小，人生促，
　这潮却能载我去远方；
　　过了沙洲后，
　但愿当面见**领航**。

R. 勃朗宁 (1812—1889)

夜会

　灰濛濛海面，黑幽幽长岸；
　低低挂着的半月黄又大；
　梦中惊醒的浪花在蹦跳，
　像无数小小的光环闪耀——
　当我急行的船擦着淤沙，
　减慢了速度进了小海湾。

　三里路沙滩海香暖风轻；
　过了三块地，来到那农家；

A tap at the pane, the quick sharp scratch

And blue spurt of a lighted match,

And a voice less loud, thro' it's joys and fears

Than the two hearts beating each to each!

EMILY BRONTË

The Old Stoic

Riches I hold in light esteem,

And love I laugh to scorn;

And lust of fame was but a dream

That vanished with the morn:

And if I pray, the only prayer

That moves my lips for me

Is, 'Leave the heart that I bear,

And give me liberty!'

Yes, as my swift days near their goal,

'Tis all that I implore —

Through life and death a chainless soul,

With courage to endure.

一叩窗,顿时刮嚓一声响——
火柴迸出了蓝荧荧火光;
饱含喜乐惊怕的悄悄话
轻过怦怦对跳的两颗心!

艾米莉·勃朗特 (1818—1848)

坚忍澹泊的长者

对财富我并不尊重崇敬,
对爱情我嘲笑轻视;
对声名的渴求不过是梦——
黎明到来时就消失。

要是我祈祷,只有这祷词
才能够让我说出口:
"请把我的心留给我自己,
还有,请给我自由。"

当我的日子向终点驰近,
我提出唯一的请求:
生和死拴不住我的灵魂——
有勇气坚持和忍受。

ARTHUR HUGH CLOUGH

'Say Not, the Struggle Naught Availeth'

Say not, the struggle naught availeth,
    The labour and the wounds are vain,
The enemy faints not, nor faileth,
    And as things have been they remain.

If hopes were dupes, fears may be liars;
    It may be, in yon smoke concealed,
Your comrades chase e'en now the fliers,
    And, but for you, possess the field.

For while the tired waves, vainly breaking,
    Seem here no painful inch to gain,
Far back, through creeks, and inlets making,
    Comes silent, flooding in, the main.

And not by eastern windows only,
    When daylight comes, comes in the light,
In front, the sun climbs slow, how slowly,
    But westward, look, the land is bright.

克拉夫 (1819—1861)

"不要说斗争没什么用处"

不要说斗争没什么用处,
　只是白白地辛苦和受伤;
别说敌人没打昏没打输——
　一切同以前没什么两样。

希望倘受骗,骗子是惊慌;
　要不是你,在那处硝烟里
你战友也许控制了战场,
　眼下还甚至在追杀逃敌。

别看这里的倦波空拍岸,
　似乎一寸地也很难漫到;
在内陆,那些河汊与河湾
　悄悄中已满是大海来潮。

每天当白昼到来的时候,
　光线不只是照进了东窗;
正面看,太阳升得慢悠悠,
　但是朝西看,大地已亮堂。

DANTE GABRIEL ROSSETTI

Three Shadows

I looked and saw your eyes
    In the shadow of your hair
As a traveller sees the stream
    In the shadow of the wood;
And I said, 'My faint heart sighs
    Ah me! to linger there,
To drink deep and to dream
    In that sweet solitude.'

I looked and saw your heart
    In the shadow of your eyes,
As a seeker sees the gold
    In the shadow of the stream;
And I said, 'Ah me! what art
    Should win the immortal prize,
Whose want must make life cold
    And Heaven a hollow dream?'

I looked and saw your love
    In the shadow of your heart,

D. G. 罗塞蒂 (1828—1882)

三重影

在你秀发的暗影里
　我看见了你的明眸,
犹如在林木暗影中
　跋涉者看见了溪水;
我疲惫的心在叹息,
　说是要在那里逗留,
在那甜美的僻静中
　畅饮后在梦乡沉睡。

在你眼睛的暗影里
　我看见你的一颗心,
犹如在溪水暗影中
　淘金者看见了金沙;
我说,"要怎样的技艺
　可赢得那不朽奖品——
缺了它,人生被冷冻,
　天堂是说梦的空话。"

在你心灵的暗影里,
　我看见你心中的爱,

As a diver sees the pearl

　　　　In the shadow of the sea;

And I murmured, not above

　　My breath, but all apart,—

'Ah! you can love, true girl,

　　And is your love for me?'[1]

CHRISTINA ROSSETTI

A Birthday

My heart is like a singing bird

　　Whose nest is in a watered shoot;

My heart is like an apple tree

　　Whose boughs are bent with thickset fruit;

My heart is like a rainbow shell

　　That paddles in a halcyon sea;

My heart is gladder than all these

　　Because my love is come to me.

1　本诗中，各诗节的韵式为 abcdabcd，在这一行的译文中没有做到。

犹如在海水暗影下
　　采珠人看见了珍珠;

我悄没声儿在低语,
　　但字字都能听明白:
"你能爱,纯洁的姑娘啊,
　　你的爱是不是给我?"

克里斯蒂娜·罗塞蒂 (1830—1894)

生日

我的心像是歌唱的小鸟,
　　筑窝的嫩枝上雨润露滋;
我的心如同一棵苹果树,
　　累累的果实挂弯了树枝;
我的心好似斑斓的海螺,
　　浮游在波浪不兴的海上;
我的心比所有这些都欢,
　　因为我爱人来到了身旁。

Raise me a dais of silk and down;
    Hang it with vair and purple dyes;
Carve it in doves, and pomegranates,
    And peacocks with a hundred eyes;
Work it in gold and silver grapes,
    In leaves, and silver fleurs-de-lys;
Because the birthday of my life
    Is come, my love is come to me.

WILLIAM MORRIS

Love Is Enough

Love is enough: though the world be a-waning,
And the woods have no voice but the voice of complaining,
    Though the sky be too dark for dim eyes to discover
The gold-cups and daisies fair blooming thereunder,
Though the hills be held shadows, and the sea a dark wonder,
    And this day draw a veil over all deeds pass'd over,
Yet their hands shall not tremble, their feet shall not falter;
The void shall not weary, the fear shall not alter
    These lips and these eyes of the loved and the lover.

放好我绸缎羽绒的高座；
　　用毛皮和紫色为它装点；
刻上带着百翎斑的孔雀，
　　饰上野鸽子和石榴图案；
再做上镶金嵌银的葡萄，
　　做上叶瓣和纯银百合花；
我的人生也有了个生日，
　　因为我心上那个人来啦。

W. 莫里斯 (1834—1896)

爱就已足够

爱就已足够：任世界在变暗，
任树林的声音里全都是悲叹，
　　任天空漆黑得让倦眼看不到
天下盛开着的金盏花和雏菊；
任山岭成暗影或大海黑黢黢，
　　任这天拉上幕把往事都遮掉，
他们手不会抖，脚依然坚定，
那彼此相爱者的嘴唇和眼睛，
　　连空虚和恐惧，都改变不了。

ALGERNON CHARLES SWINBURNE

'Love Laid His Sleepless Head'

Love laid his sleepless head
On a thorny rosy bed;
And his eyes with tears were red,
And pale his lips as the dead.

And fear and sorrow and scorn
Kept watch by his head forlorn,
Till the night was overworn,
And the world was merry with morn.

And Joy came up with the day,
And kissed Love's lips as he lay,
And the watchers ghostly and gray
Sped from his pillow away.

And his eyes as the dawn grew bright,
And his lips waxed ruddy as light:
Sorrow may reign for a night,
But day shall bring back delight.[1]

1　本诗这样的四行一韵并不多见。

斯温伯恩 (1837—1909)

"没法睡着觉的爱神"

没法睡着觉的爱神
靠着多刺的玫瑰枕；
眼睛因流泪而通红，
嘴唇苍白得像死人。

恐惧和藐视和悲伤
守在他孤凄的头旁，
直守到夜尽见曙光，
黎明叫世界喜洋洋。

欢乐的早晨吻了吻
躺卧中爱神的嘴唇，
三个鬼看守忙转身，
灰溜溜逃离了爱神。

他眼睛随天色变亮，
他嘴唇渐渐泛红光：
悲伤虽得逞一晚上，
但白天总带回欢畅。

AUSTIN DOBSON

In After Days[1]

In after days when grasses high
O'er-top the stone where I shall lie,
   Though ill or well the world adjust
   My slender claim to honoured dust,
I shall not question or reply.

I shall not see the morning sky;
I shall not hear the nightwind's sigh;
   I shall be mute, as all men must
      In after days!

But yet, now living, fain were I
That someone then should testify,
   Saying—'He held his pen in trust
   To Art, not serving shame or lust.'
Will none?—Then let my memory die
      In after days!

---

[1] 这种韵式为 aabba aabR aabbaR 的诗体是典型的 rondeau（回旋诗），这种三段两韵诗常见于法国谣曲，每行八音节四音步。R 是 refrain 缩写，意为叠句，常是第一行前半部分。

多布森 (1840—1921)

在身后的日子里

当草在我身后的日子里
长得高过了盖我的碑石,
   我遗骸要求的那点尊重
   任世人答应还是不答应,
我不会答话或提出问题。

我将看不见空中的晨曦;
我将听不见夜风的叹息;
   我得像别人一样不出声
   在身后的日子里!

可现在活着的我倒愿意
那时会有人出来说一句:
   "当初他的笔对艺术忠诚,
   从没把污秽和贪欲侍奉。"
没人说? 那就别把我回忆
   在身后的日子里!

THOMAS HARDY

'Ah, Are You Digging on My Grave'

'Ah, are you digging on my grave
    My loved one?—planting rue?'
—'No: yesterday he went to wed
One of the brightest wealth has bred.
"It cannot hurt her now," he said,
    "That I should not be true."'

'Then who is digging in my grave?
    My nearest dearest kin?'
—'Ah, no; they sit and think, "What use
What good will planting flowers produce?
No tendance of her mound can loose
    Her spirit from Death's gin."'

'But some one digs upon my grave?
    My enemy?—prodding sly?'
—'Nay: When she heard you had passed the Gate
That shuts on all flesh soon or late,
She thought you no more worth her hate,
    And cares not where you lie.'

哈代 (1840—1928)

"哦，你这是在刨我的坟土"

"哦，你这是在刨我的坟土？
　　亲爱的，要种苦芸香？"
——"不，你那人昨天成了亲，
娶的是大财主家的千金。
'就算我现在已经变了心，
　　对她没伤害，'他讲。"

"那么又是谁刨我的坟土？
　　是我最亲近的亲人？"
——"哦不，他们坐那里寻思：
'种种花能种出什么好事？
死了的不可能再回人世——
　　任怎么照料她的坟。'"

"但确实有谁刨我的坟土——
　　是对手暗中施诡计？"
——"不，她听说你过了那道门，
知道人迟早都有这命运，
认为不值得再把你怀恨，
　　不在乎你埋在哪里。"

'Then, who is digging on my grave?
　　Say—since I have not guessed!'
—'O it is I, my mistress dear,
Your little dog, who still lives near,
And much I hope my movements here
　　Have not disturbed your rest?'

'Ah, yes! You dig upon my grave…
　　Why flashed it not on me
That one true heart was left behind!
What feeling do we ever find
In equal among human kind
　　A dog's fidelity!'

'Mistress, I dug upon your grave
　　To bury a bone, in case
I should be hungry near this spot
When passing on my daily trot.
I am sorry, but I quite forgot
　　It was your resting-place.'

"那究竟谁在刨我的坟土?
　　你说吧,我已没法猜!"
——"哦,是我呀,亲爱的女主人,
是你的小狗,仍住在附近;
我希望我在这里的活动
　　对你的安息没妨碍。"

"哦,是你呀在刨我的坟土……
　　为什么我竟没想到
世上还留一颗忠诚的心!
人类中是否有什么感情
能比得上一条狗的忠诚——
　　依我看恐怕很难找!"

"女主人,我来刨你的坟土,
　　要埋根骨头在这里;
每天我都要跑过这地方——
这样可免得有时饿得慌。
真是抱歉,我竟然就遗忘
　　这里是你的安息地。"

ROBERT BRIDGES

'When First We Meet We Did Not Guess'[1]

When first we met we did not guess

That Love would prove so hard a master;

Of more than common friendliness

When first we met we did not guess.

Who could foretell this sore distress,

This irretrievable disaster

When first we met?—We did not guess

That Love would prove so hard a master.

WILLIAM ERNEST HENLEY

Invictus[2]

Out of the night that covers me,
 Black as the Pit from pole to pole,[3]
I thank whatever gods may be
 For my unconquerable soul.

---

1 这是来自法国的 triolet（特利奥莱八行二韵，第一行在第四、第七行重复，第二行在第八行重复）。
2 invictus 是拉丁文，意为 unconquered。
3 据《神曲》中的说法，地狱是贯通北极与南极的大黑坑。

布里吉斯 (1844—1930)

"我们初见时哪能料到"

我们初见时哪能料到
爱神竟是这么狠的霸王!
原以为只是泛泛之交:
我们初见时哪能料到!
谁能预料这样的苦恼
和这种没法补救的灾殃?
我们初见时,哪能料到
爱神竟是这样狠的霸王!

亨利 (1849—1903)

不屈不挠

地狱般夜色一片黑沉沉,
　　在那笼罩下我高声喊话:
哪位神给我不屈的灵魂,
　　无论他是谁我都感谢他。

In the fell clutch of circumstance

    I have not winced nor cried aloud.

Under the bludgeonings of chance

    My head is bloody, but unbowed.

Beyond this place of wrath and tears

    Looms but the Horror of the shade,

And yet the menace of the years

    Finds, and shall find, me unafraid.

It matters not how strait the gate,

    How charged with punishments the scroll,

I am the master of my fate:

    I am the captain of my soul.

ROBERT LOUIS STEVENSON

Requiem

Under the wide and starry sky,

Dig the grave and let me lie.

Glad did I live and gladly die,

    And I laid me down with a will.

凶恶的境遇一把抓牢我,
　　我没有哭叫也没有退后;
命运的大棒连连猛击我,
　　我满头是血但决不低头。

这世间充满严酷与泪水,
　　恐怖的阴司又黑影幢幢;
但任凭岁月逞它的淫威,
　　我现在将来都不会惊恐。

不管那永生之门多狭窄,
　　不管天书上把刑罚载满,
我是我自己命运的主宰,
　　我是自己灵魂的指挥官。

斯蒂文森 (1850—1894)

挽歌

满是星斗的昊天之下,
挖一个墓坑让我躺下,
我生也欢乐死也欢洽,
　　躺下的时候有个遗愿。

This be the verse you grave for me:
Here he lies where he longed to be,
Home is the sailor, home from sea,
 And the hunter home from the hill.

OSCAR WILDE

In the Gold Room (A Harmony)

Her ivory hands on the ivory keys
 Strayed in a fitful fantasy,
Like the silver gleam when the poplar trees
 Rustle their pale leaves listlessly,
 Or the drifting foam of a restless sea
When the waves show their teeth in the flying breeze.

Her gold hair fell on the wall of gold
 Like the delicate gossamer tangles spun
On the burnished disk of the marigold,
 Or the sun-flower turning to meet the sun
 When the gloom of the dark blue night is done,
And the spear of the lily is aureoled.

几行诗句请替我刻上:
他躺在他想望的地方;
海上的水手回到故乡,
　　下山的猎手进了家园。

王尔德 (1854—1900)

在金色房间里(一段和声)

象牙般的手弹着象牙色琴键,
　　漫游在一阵一阵幻想里,
像白杨倦怠地晃动浅色叶片,
　　沙沙声中闪着银光熠熠,
　　或像疾风下浪涛露牙时
汹涌的海面上水沫飘洒四溅。

她的金头发飘拂在金色墙上,
　　像是金盏花的锃亮花朵
缠着纤细光洁的蛛丝结的网,
　　又像黑中带蓝的夜刚过,
　　向日葵转身朝太阳望着,
或像百合嫩芽外的一圈金光。

And her sweet red lips on these lips of mine

    Burned like the ruby fire set

In the swinging lamp of a crimson shrine,

    Or the bleeding wounds of the pomegranate,

    Or the heart of the lotus drenched and wet

With the spilt-out blood of the rose-red wine.

ALFRED EDWARD HOUSMAN

Loveliest of Trees

Loveliest of trees, the cherry now

Is hung with bloom along the bough,

And stands about the woodland ride

Wearing white for Eastertide.[1]

Now, of my threescore years and ten,[2]

Twenty will not come again,

And take from seventy springs a score,

It only leaves me fifty more.

---

1 Eastertide 指的是从复活节起到其后 40 天（或 57 天）之间的节期。
2 《旧约全书·诗篇》90 章 10 节中说：The days of our years are three score years and ten。

而她甜蜜的红唇在我嘴唇上，
　　灼热得像是绯红神龛里
那盏吊灯中红宝石般的火光，
　　或像石榴的创伤滴着血，
　　又如鲜血般玫瑰红酒里
浸得湿淋淋的睡莲的心一样。

豪斯曼 (1859—1936)

最可爱的树

最可爱的树要数樱桃，
眼下它花儿正满枝梢，
复活节期间披着素装，
站在林间的小路边上。

在我可期的七十岁内，
有二十已经一去不回；
七十中把这二十削减，
就只剩下五十度春天。

And since to look at things in bloom

Fifty springs are little room,

About the woodlands I will go

To see the cherry hang with snow.

MARY COLERIDGE

Slowly[1]

Heavy is my heart,

 Dark are thine eyes.

Thou and I must part

 Ere the sun rise.

Ere the sun rise

 Thou and I must part.

Dark are thine eyes,

 Heavy is my heart.

---

1 这首诗有点像回文诗,但其回文并非以字为单位。

要把盛开的东西观赏,

五十度春天实在不长;

我要把那片林地走遍,

把披着雪的樱桃看看。

玛丽·柯尔律治 (1861—1907)

意迟迟

我心儿多沉郁,

　你眼光多暗淡。

你和我得分离

　在太阳升起前。

在太阳升起前

　你和我得分离。

你眼光多暗淡,

　我心儿多沉郁。

WILLIAM BUTLER YEATS

'Down by the Salley Gardens'

Down by the salley gardens my love and I did meet;
She passed the salley gardens with little snow-white feet.
She bid me take love easy, as the leaves grow on the tree;
But I, being young and foolish, with her would not agree.

In a field by the river my love and I did stand,
And on my leaning shoulder she laid her snow-white hand.
She bid me take life easy, as the grass grows on the weirs;
But I was young and foolish and now am full of tears.

RUDYARD KIPLING

Coward[1]

I could not look on Death, which being known,
Men led me to him, blindfold and alone.

1　吉卜林为第一次世界大战阵亡者写墓铭体作品。这里他写一名军人自述因怯战而被处决的情景。这首对句曾被《简明不列颠百科全书》（1985）中"诗"这一条目用作例子。

叶芝 (1865—1939)

"在那些杨柳园子边"

在那些杨柳园子边我爱人同我会面；
她那双纤小雪白的脚走过了杨柳园。
她叫我把爱情看淡点，像树长出绿叶；
但是我年轻无知，她的话我并不同意。

我的爱人同我伫立在河边的田野上，
她雪白的手搭在我依偎着她的肩膀。
她叫我把人生看淡点，像堰上长青草；
但是我年轻无知，到如今却泪水直掉。

吉卜林 (1865—1936)

胆小鬼

我未能正视死神；人们一觉察，
便蒙住我眼睛，单送我去见他。

ERNEST DOWSON

Cynara

Non sum qualis eram bonae sub regno Cynarai[1]

Last night, ah, yesternight, betwixt her lips and mine
There fell thy shadow, Cynara! thy breath was shed
Upon my soul between the kisses and the wine;
And I was desolate and sick of an old passion,
　Yea, I was desolate and bowed my head:
I have been faithful to thee, Cynara! in my fashion.

All night upon mine heart I felt her warm heart beat,
Night-long within mine arms in love and sleep she lay;
Surely the kisses of her bought red mouth were sweet;
But I was desolate and sick of an old passion,
　When I awoke and found the dawn was gray:
I have been faithful to thee, Cynara! in my fashion.

1　拉丁文，出自古罗马诗人贺拉斯（公元前65—前8）《颂诗》中诗人对维纳斯的求告。

道森 (1867—1900)

希娜拉

我已不是希娜拉主宰下的我

昨晚上,昨晚上在她和我的嘴唇当中
落下了你影子,希娜拉!在酒和吻之间
你幽幽呼出的气息,掩上了我的灵魂;
于是,那一缕旧情使得我难受又孤凄,
　是啊,我满心孤凄,头低到胸前:
希娜拉!我一直以我的方式忠实于你。

一整夜,她温暖的心贴着我的心在跳,
整夜里,我感到她怀着爱睡在我怀中;
我从她红唇上买来的吻,当然很美妙;
但是,那一缕旧情使得我难受又孤凄——
　每当我醒来时看到曙色灰蒙蒙:
希娜拉!我一直以我的方式忠实于你。

I have forgot much, Cynara! gone with the wind,[1]

Flung roses, roses riotously with the throng,

Dancing, to put thy pale, lost lilies out of mind;

But I was desolate and sick of an old passion,

 Yea, all the time, because the dance was long:

I have been faithful to thee, Cynara! in my fashion.

I cried for madder music and for stronger wine,

But when the feast is finished and the lamps expire,

Then falls thy shadow, Cynara! the night is thine;

And I am desolate and sick of an old passion,

 Yea, hungry for the lips of my desire:

I have been faithful to thee, Cynara! in my fashion.

WILLIAM HENRY DAVIES

Leisure

What is this life if, full of care,

We have no time to stand and stare.

1　Gone with the wind 可译为"随风而去"或"俱往矣"等。这短语后被美国女作家玛格丽特·米切尔（1900—1949）用作书名——中译本为《乱世佳人》或《飘》。

希娜拉！我忘了多少风流云散的事情，
忘了抛着玫瑰跳着舞，在人群中喧嚷，
要把你苍白的失落百合逐出我的心；
但是，那一缕旧情使得我难受又孤凄，
　　是啊，因为舞得久，一直是这样：
希娜拉！我一直以我的方式忠实于你。

我呼喊着，要更疯狂的音乐更烈的酒，
但是当盛宴结束，当灯火一盏盏熄掉，
你的影子就降下，希娜拉！夜归你所有；
于是，那一缕旧情使得我难受又孤凄，
　　是啊，为想望那双唇我备受煎熬：
希娜拉！我一直以我的方式忠实于你。

戴维斯 (1871—1940)

闲暇

这哪算生活：若满腹心事，
没时间站停了久久凝视。

No time to stand beneath the boughs

And stare as long as sheep or cows.

No time to see, when woods we pass,

Where squirrels hide their nuts in grass.

No time to see, in broad daylight,

Streams full of stars, like skies at night.

No time to turn at Beauty's glance,

And watch her feet, how they can dance.

No time to wait till her mouth can

Enrich that smile her eyes began.

A poor life this if, full of care,

We have no time to stand and stare.

没时间站停在树枝下面,
像牛羊那样长时间观看。

没时间观看,松鼠在林中
把坚果藏进哪一处草丛。

没时间看阳光下的小河
像夜空的繁星闪闪烁烁。

没时间转身看美人顾盼,
观赏她那双脚舞姿翩翩。

没时间等一等,让她的嘴
使她眼中的笑意更完美。

这生活真惨:若满腹心事,
没时间站停了久久凝视。

RALPH HODGSON

Stupidity Street

I saw with open eyes

Singing birds sweet

Sold in the shops

For the people to eat,

Sold in the shops of

Stupidity Street.

I saw in vision

The worm in the wheat,

And in the shops nothing

For people to eat;

Nothing for sale in

Stupidity Street.

WALTER DE LA MARE

Silver

Slowly, silently, now the moon

Walks the night in her silver shoon;

霍奇森 (1871—1962)

愚蠢街

我眼睁睁看着
可爱的鸣禽
在店里被出售,
给人做食品;
店家的那条街,
愚蠢是街名。

我仿佛也看见
麦上长满虫,
而家家商店里
没食物供应;
在那条愚蠢街
已没有货品。

德拉梅尔 (1873—1956)

银

现在月亮穿一双银色鞋
慢慢地静静地走进了夜;

This way, and that, she peers, and sees

Silver fruit upon silver trees;

One by one the casements catch

Her beams beneath the silver thatch;

Couched in his kennel, like a log,

With paws of silver sleeps the dog;

From their shadowy cote the white breasts peep

Of doves in a silver-feathered sleep;

A harvest mouse goes scampering by,

With silver claws, and silver eye;

And motionless fish in the water gleam,

By silver reeds in a silver stream.

JOHN MASEFIELD

Sea-Fever

I must go down to the seas again, to the lonely sea and the sky,

And all I ask is a tall ship and a star to steer her by,

And the wheel's kick and the wind's song and the white sail's shaking,

And a grey mist on the sea's face and a grey dawn breaking.

向这儿望望，朝那里瞧瞧，

看到银果子挂在银树梢；

银色草屋顶下一扇扇窗，

一个接一个框住她的光；

在窝里趴着银脚爪的狗

睡得昏沉沉像一段木头；

幽暗的棚里白胸脯显现，

是鸽子裹在银羽里安眠；

收获时的田鼠匆匆跑过——

银爪子铮亮，银眼睛闪烁；

银色溪流中，银色芦苇旁，

鱼一动不动，在水中闪光。

梅斯菲尔德 (1878—1967)

恋海热

我得重下海去，去那长天下寂寥的大海，

我只要一颗星为我导航，只要桅高船快，

只要海风的歌唱、白帆的震颤、舵轮的倔强，

只要海面上灰濛濛雾霭，灰蒙蒙破晓曙光。

I must go down to the seas again, for the call of the running tide[1]

Is a wild call and a clear call that may not be denied;

And all I ask is a windy day with the white clouds flying,

And the flung spray and the blown spume, and the sea-gulls crying.

I must go down to the seas again, to the vagrant gypsy life,

To the gull's way and the whale's way where the wind's like a whetted knife;

And all I ask is a merry yarn from a laughing fellow-rover,

And quiet sleep and a sweet dream when the long trick's over.

JOSEPH CAMPBELL

The Old Woman

As a white candle
　In a holy place,
So is the beauty
　Of an aged face.

As the spent radiance
　Of the winter sun,

---

[1] 此处指落潮,因为船舶一般都在落潮时启航。

我得重下海去,因为海潮在奔流澎湃,
那种召唤清晰又豪迈,叫人没法再等待,
我只要白天里疾风劲吹,吹得白云飞翔,
只要喷溅的水花、飘洒的浪沫、海鸥的叫嚷。

我得重下海去,过得像漂泊的吉卜赛人自在,
去海鸥和长鲸出没的所在,任海风快刀般吹来,
我只要有欢笑的旅伴,把快活的海外奇谭讲讲,
只要长久的操舵后,静静的安睡,甜甜的梦乡。

J. 坎贝尔 (1879—1944)

老妇

一支白蜡烛
　　点在圣坛上,
同样美的是
　　上年纪的面庞。

冬日的斜阳
　　热尽光也微,

So is a woman

    With her travail done,

Her brood gone from her,

    And her thoughts as still

As the waters

    Under a ruined mill.

JAMES STEPHENS

The Snare

I hear a sudden cry of pain!

    There is a rabbit in a snare;

Now I hear the cry again,

    But I cannot tell from where.[1]

    But I cannot tell from where

He is calling out for aid!

    Crying on the frightened air,

Making everything afraid!

1　本诗每个诗节的最末一行总是下一诗节的第一行，这一点是比较特殊的。

尽瘁的妇女
　　有那样的余晖。

儿女全离去，
　　心情也安恬，
像一塘清水
　　在废弃磨坊前。

斯蒂芬斯 (1882—1950)

机关

突然我听到痛苦的惨叫！
　　是有只兔子夹在机关里；
现在这惨叫我再次听到，
　　但是不知道这发自哪里。

　　但是不知道这发自哪里，
尽管这呼叫是请求救助！
　　受惊的空气传来这呼吁，
让所有的一切感到恐怖！

Making everything afraid!

    Wrinkling up his little face!

As he cries again for aid;

    —And I cannot find the place!

And I cannot find the place

Where his paw is in the snare!

    Little one! Oh, Little One!

I am searching everywhere!

JAMES JOYCE

'O Sweetheart, Hear You'

O sweetheart, hear you

    Your lover's tale;

A man shall have sorrow

    When friends him fail.

For he shall know then

    Friends be untrue

And a little ashes

    Their words come to.

让所有的一切感到恐怖!
　　他准是痛得扭歪了小脸——
当他再一次高呼着求助!
　　而我却找不到那个地点!

　　而我却找不到那个地点,
可是他的脚夹在机关里!
　　啊,小家伙,可怜的小家伙!
我正在到处搜索寻找你!

乔伊斯 (1882—1941)

"心上人,听听你"

心上人,听听你
　　情人的故事;
他吃了朋友亏
　　自然会忧戚。

到这时他看清
　　朋友不忠信,
他们间的誓言
　　变一撮灰烬。

But one unto him

    Will softly move

And softly woo him

    In ways of love.

His hand is under

    Her smooth round breast;

So he who has sorrow

    Shall have rest.

DAVID HERBERT LAWRENCE

Green

The dawn was apple-green,

    The sky was green wine held up in the sun,

The moon was a golden petal between.

She opened her eyes, and green

    They shone, clear like flowers undone

For the first time, now for the first time seen.

但有人会过来
  轻轻靠拢他,
怀着爱轻轻地
  倾吐着情话。

姑娘的腰肢柔,
  他双手一搂,
就得到了安宁,
  也就消了愁。

劳伦斯 (1885—1930)

绿

曙色是苹果绿一片,
  天空是绿酒高擎在阳光下,
月亮是两者间的金色花瓣。

她睁开眼来,那双眼
  绿莹莹,明净得就像两朵花
初次开放,如今初次被看见。

EDWIN MUIR

The Castle

All through that summer at ease we lay,

And daily from the turret wall

We watched the mowers in the hay

And the enemy half a mile away.

They seemed no threat to us at all.

For what, we thought had we to fear

With our arms and provender, load on load,

Our towering battlements, tier on tier,

And friendly allies drawing near

On every leafy summer road.

Our gates are strong, our wall were thick,

So smooth and high, no man could win

A foothold there, no clever trick

Could take us, have us dead or quick.

Only a bird could have got in.

What could they offer us for bait?

Our captain was brave and we were true....

缪尔 (1887—1959)

城堡

那一夏天我们睡得自在,
每天都登上塔楼望四野,
只见农夫割下了草在晒,
而敌人还在半英里之外——
看起来对我们绝无威胁。

我们备足了武器和粮草,
高耸的城垛一层又一层,
沿每条多树的夏日大道
我们的友军不久将开到——
我们想,还有什么要担心!

堡门既坚固,堡墙又厚实,
又高又平的墙面难落脚,
对我们,任谁也无计可施——
难于抓活的,难叫我们死,
能进我们城堡的只有鸟。

他们用什么能引诱我们?
我们既忠诚,长官又豪迈。……

There was a little private gate,

A little wicked wicket gate.

The wizened warder let them through.

Oh then our maze of tunneled stone

Grew thin and treacherous as air.

The cause was lost without a groan,

The famous citadel overthrown,

And all its secret galleries bare.

How can this shameful tale be told?

I will maintain until my death

We could do nothing, being sold;

Our only enemy was gold,

And we had no arms to fight it with.

但是有一扇小小的便门,
一扇丑陋枯朽的小后门,
枯瘪的看守放他们进来。

我们迷宫似的石头城堡
变得空气般稀薄而凶险。
还没哼一声就全盘输掉
这著名的要塞就此毁掉,
隐蔽的坑道全都见了天。

这可耻故事怎么告诉人?
既然被出卖,还能干点啥!
这一点我到死也要重申:
我们唯一的敌人是黄金,
我们没一件武器对付它。

THOMAS STEARNS ELIOT

Cat Morgan Introduces Himself[1]

I once was a Pirate what sailed the 'igh seas —[2]
    But now I've retired as a com-mission-aire:
And that's how you find me a-takin' my ease
    And keepin' the door in a Bloomsbury Square.[3]

I'm partial to partridges, likewise to grouse,
    And I favour that Devonshire cream in a bowl;
But I'm allus content with a drink on the 'ouse
    And a bit o' cold fish when I done me patrol.

I ain't got much polish, me manners is gruff,
    But I've got a good coat, and I keep meself smart;
And everyone says, and I guess that's enough;
    'You can't but like Morgan, 'e's got a kind 'art.'

---

1 爱猫的作者身为教父，在给教子们的信中常夹有他写的"猫诗"，这些诗 1939 年由 Faber and Faber 公司出版，名为 *Old Possum's Book of Practical Cats*。本诗为其中最后一首，是 1952 年版中加的。1981 年，Andrew Lloyd Webber (1948—) 将之编成音乐剧，在伦敦上演大获成功，风行至今，曾来我国及世界各地演出。
2 本诗有打油性质，语法、用词、拼写等都不很规范，例如这里的 'igh = high 等。
3 布卢姆斯伯里区是二十世纪初伦敦的文化艺术中心，作者任总编的费柏出版公司在该区的 Russell 广场。

艾略特 (1888—1965)

摩根猫的自我介绍

我一度是个横行海上的强盗,
　后来洗手不干就当了看门人:
所以你看到我舒舒服服睡觉——
　一边在布卢姆斯伯里守守门。

我爱吃山鹑,同样也爱吃松鸡,
　喜欢就着碗吃点德文郡奶油;
经常喝免费饮料最合我心意,
　巡查回来吃冷鱼也对我胃口。

我没有修养,言谈举止很粗鲁,
　但是一身好外套让我很体面;
而大家说的这句话叫我满足:
　摩根心眼好,叫你不能不喜欢。

I got knocked about on the Barbary Coast,[1]

 And me voice it ain't no sich melliferous horgan;

But yet I can state, and I'm not one to boast,

 That some of the gals is dead keen on old Morgan.[2]

So if you 'ave business with Faber - or Faber —[3]

 I'll give you this tip, and it's worth a lot more:

You'll save yourself time, and you'll spare yourself labour

 If jist you make friends with the Cat at the door.

HUGH MACDIARMID

The Storm-Cock's Song[4]

My song today is the storm-cock's song.

When the cold winds blow and the driving snow

Hides the tree-tops, only his song rings out

In the lulls in the storm, so let mine go!

---

1 巴巴里海岸指埃及以西的北非沿海地区，以前多海盗；又指 1906 年大地震前美国旧金山沿岸，那里多赌场妓院。

2 Cat 中间加 p 就成为 Capt. Morgan，可指著名威尔士海盗 Sir Henry Morgan（有一种朗姆酒以此为商标）。

3 Faber and Faber 为著名出版公司，其作者中有十多位诺贝尔文学奖得主（包括本诗作者），这里摩根猫将 and 误拼为 or。

4 Storm-Cock 也叫田鹎，同海燕等飞禽一样，被认为能预报风暴等坏天气。

我曾在巴巴里海岸流浪漂泊，
　　我嗓音一点不像柔润的风琴——
我一向不爱吹牛，但是可以说：
　　有些姑娘对老摩根爱得要命。

所以你若同费柏公司打交道，
　　我给你透个大有价值的秘密：
只要好好地结交我这看门猫，
　　你就能节省时间又不花力气。

麦克迪尔米德 (1892—1978)

大鸫之歌

今天我的歌是大鸫的歌。
当冷风劲吹，狂舞的雪花
遮没了树顶，而风雪略一停，
只有它高唱：我也这么唱吧！

On the topmost twig of a leafless ash

As sits bolt upright against the sky

Surveying the white fields and the leafless woods

And distant red in the East with his buoyant eye,

Surely he has little enough cause to sing

When even the hedgerow berries are already pulped by the frost

Or eaten by other birds — yet alone and aloft

To another hungry day his greeting is tossed.

Blessed are those who have songs to sing

When others are silent; poor song though it be,

Just a message to the silence that someone is still

Alive and glad, though on a naked tree.

What if it is only a few churning notes

Flung out in a loud and artless way?

His 'will I do it? Do it I will!' is worth a lot

Where the rest have nothing at all to say.

它昂然栖在光秃秃桤树上，
在树顶小树枝上衬着天空，
含希望的眼睛审视着秃林、
白茫茫田野和遥远的东方殷红。

其实没什么可以让它唱——
甚至连树篱上的浆果也被霜冻坏
或被别的鸟吃掉，而它却在高处
独自欢迎又一个饥饿日到来。

当人家不作声，有歌要唱的
就非常幸运，尽管唱得不漂亮，
这是给无声一个信息：仍有谁
高兴地活着，即使待在秃树上。

哪怕它叫出的几声响亮音符
搅在一起并不妙，有什么关系？
当人家不出声，它那"我可要干？
可我要干！"却有着很大意义。

ROBERT GRAVES

The Face in the Mirror

Gray haunted eyes, absent mindedly glaring

From wide, uneven orbits; one brow drooping

Somewhat over the eye

Because of a missile fragment still inhering

Skin deep, as a foolish record of old-world fighting.

Crookedly broken nose—low tackling caused it;

Cheeks, furrowed; coarse gray hair, flying frenetic;

Forehead, wrinkled and high;

Jowls, prominent; ears, large; jaw, pugilistic;

Teeth, few; lips, full and ruddy; mouth, ascetic.

I pause with razor poised, scowling derision

At the mirrored man whose beard needs my attention,

And once more ask him why

He still stands ready, with a boy's presumption,

To court the queen in her high silk pavilion.

格雷夫斯 (1895—1985)

镜中的脸

带愁的灰眼睛干瞪着,走神的目光
发自不对称的宽眼窝;一只眼睛上
像耷拉着一条眉毛,
因为有弹片在浅浅的皮肉里埋藏,
记录了旧世界里那场争斗的混账。

踢球时因被恶意阻截而摔坏的鼻子;
两颊沟纹深;头发白而粗,飘拂得癫痴;
额头皱纹多,显得高;
颌部突,耳朵大,下巴同拳击手的相似;
牙没剩几颗,双唇厚又红;嘴像在禁食。

我停下手中举着的剃刀,皱起了眉头
笑话镜中人,他胡子需要我经常侍候;
我再一次向他问道:
为什么他总是像男孩似的心高皮厚,
总准备把绸帐篷里的高贵女王追求。

ROY CAMPBELL

Autumn

I love to see, when leaves depart,

The clear anatomy arrive,

Winter, the paragon of art,

That kills all forms of life and feeling[1]

Save what is pure and will survive.

Already now the clanging chains

Of geese are harnessed to the moon:

Stripped are the great sun-clouding planes:

And the dark pines, their own revealing,

Let in the needles of the noon.

Strained by the gale the olives whiten

Like hoary wrestlers bent with toil

And, with the vines, their branches lighten

To brim our vats where summer lingers

In the red froth and sun-gold oil.

1　本诗韵式也较特殊，为 abacb dedce fgfhg ijihj。

R. 坎贝尔 (1901—1957)

秋

我爱看:随树叶离开枝桠
而到来的那种分明剖析——
冬天这艺术的珍品,抹杀
每一种生命的形式和感情,
幸存的只是纯真的东西。

发长喙的大雁之链,如今
已套上挽具,拴到月亮上;
遮阳的悬铃木叶子落尽,
黑森森的松林显露出原形,
接纳了针似的正午光芒。

橄榄树一片白,顶着劲风
像是白发人弓着腰搏斗;
它们的枝柯连同葡萄藤,
卸下的重负装满桶,是盛夏
淹留其中的红沫与金油。

Soon on our hearth's reviving pyre

Their rotted stems will crumble up:

And like a ruby, panting fire,

The grape will redden on your fingers

Through the lit crystal of the cup.

CECIL DAY-LEWIS

Song: 'Come, Live with Me and Be My Love'

Come, live with me and be my love,[1]

And we will all the pleasures prove

Of peace and plenty, bed and board,

That chance employment may afford.

I'll handle dainties on the docks

And thou shalt read of summer frocks:

At evening by the sour canals

We'll hope to hear some madrigals.

---

1 见马洛那首 *The Passionate Shepherd to His Love*。对这牧歌作出反应的诗常沿用其格律并以同样的第一行开始。

不久,炉中重燃的柴堆上,
它们腐朽的枝条将皱拢;
葡萄酒将同红宝石相像——
水晶般杯盏在炉光照耀下,
喷火一样把你的手映红。

戴-刘易斯 (1904—1972)

歌:"来与我同住,做我的爱人"

来与我同住,做我的爱人;
只要打零工的钱能支撑,
我们就能安逸地住和吃,
把丰裕生活的乐趣尝试。

我去码头上搬龙肝凤脑,
你读读夏日衣裙的广告,
黄昏时沿着酸臭的运河,
我们想听听情歌或牧歌。

Care on thy maiden brow shall put

A wreath of wrinkles, and thy foot

Be shod with pain: not silken dress

But toil shall tire thy loveliness.

Hunger shall make thy modest zone

And cheat fond death of all but bone —

If these delights thy mind may move,

Then live with me and be my love.

LOUIS MACNEICE

Christina

It all began so easy
 With bricks upon the floor
Building motley houses
And knocking down your houses
 And always building more.

The doll was called Christina,
 Her under-wear was lace,
She smiled while you dressed her

忧虑将给你处女的额角
戴上皱纹的花冠，你双脚
将总是酸痛；并不是绸衣，
是劳累会拖垮你的秀丽。

饥饿将是你简朴的腰带，
骗得蠢死神只得到骨骸——
倘这些乐趣打动你的心，
就来同我住，做我的爱人。

麦克尼斯 (1907—1963)

克莉斯蒂娜

这一切开始得很容易：
　　在地上用积木一块块
造五颜六色的小房子，
又推倒你这些小房子——
　　而总是越造越多起来。

这玩偶叫克莉斯蒂娜，
　　她内衣是精细网织物，
你给她穿衣时她微笑——

And when you then undressed her

    She kept a smiling face.

Until the day she tumbled

    And broke herself in two

And her legs and arms were hollow

And her yellow head was hollow

    Behind her eyes of blue.

    ★ ★ ★

He went to bed with a lady

    Somewhere seen before,

He heard the name Christina

And suddenly saw Christina

    Dead on the nursery floor.

STEPHEN SPENDER

Word[1]

The word bites like a fish.

Shall I throw it back free

1　本诗韵式较特别，为 abbcca。

而她的脸总带着微笑,
　　任便你脱掉了她衣服。

直到她有一天跌下来,
　　一下子就跌成了两段,
只见她腿和臂是空的,
只见她黄脑袋是空的,
　　尽管有蓝眼睛在前面。

　　★　★　★

他曾在哪里见到过
　　这同他上床的女郎；
一听叫克莉斯蒂娜,
就看见克莉斯蒂娜
　　死在幼儿室地板上。

斯彭德 (1909—1995)

字眼

字眼就像鱼也会咬。
可要放它生,猛一甩

Arrowing to that sea

Where thoughts lash tail and fin?

Or shall I pull it in

To rhyme upon a dish?

DYLAN THOMAS

'Do Not Go Gentle into That Good Night'[1]

Do not go gentle into that good night,[2]

Old age should burn and rave at close of day;

Rage, rage against the dying of the light.

Though wise men at their end know dark is right,

Because their words had forked no lightning they

Do not go gentle into that good night.

1　villanelle（维拉内尔）诗体来自法国，特点是：诗行等长，第一和第三行在后面各节中轮流重复，其韵式和重复规律为：AbA₁ abA abA₁ abA abA₁ abAA₁（大写字母表示整行重复）。

2　that good night 指死亡；作者写本诗时父亲病重，他觉得死亡虽属正常，但智者、善人、狂人和严肃者都没有顺从地屈服于死亡，所以希望父亲别悄然去世，要向死亡斗争。

叫它箭似地回那海,
让思绪像鱼去蹦跶?
要不然我就钓上它,
算是韵做成菜一道?

托马斯 (1914—1953)

"不要温顺地进入那美好晚上"

不要温顺地进入那美好晚上,
白天结束时老年该燃烧,狂叫;
要怒斥,怒斥白昼亮光的消亡。

智者临终时知道黑暗虽正当,
因为话没叉出闪电,他们不要
不要温顺地进入那美好晚上。

Good men, the last wave by, crying how bright
Their frail deeds might have danced in a green bay,
Rage, rage against the dying of the light.

Wild men who caught and sang the sun in flight,
And learn, too late, they grieved it on its way,
Do not go gentle into that good night.

Grave men, near death, who see with blinding sight
Blind eyes could blaze like meteors and be gay,
Rage, rage against the dying of the light.

And you, my father, there on the sad height,
Curse, bless, me now with your fierce tears, I pray.
Do not go gentle into that good night.
Rage, rage against the dying of the light.

PHILIP LARKIN

Talking in Bed

Talking in bed ought to be easiest,
Lying together there goes back so far,

善人迎着最后一浪喊：绿湾旁
他们脆弱的事迹该朗朗舞蹈；
要怒斥，怒斥白昼亮光的消亡。

狂人攫住并歌唱飞逝的太阳，
太晚才知道使其在途中苦恼，
不要温顺地进入那美好晚上。

严肃者濒死前虽然目光迷茫，
却看到盲眼能像流星般欢耀，
要怒斥，怒斥白昼亮光的消亡。

我的父亲，在你那伤心绝顶上，
求你用热泪诅咒并为我祝祷。
不要温顺地进入那美好晚上。
要怒斥，怒斥白昼亮光的消亡。

拉金 (1922—1985)

在床上谈话

在床上谈话该是最容易的事，
躺在一起可追溯到很远很远，

An emblem of two people being honest.

Yet more and more time passes silently.

Outside, the wind's incomplete unrest

Builds and disperses clouds about the sky,

And dark towns heap up on the horizon.

None of this cares for us. Nothing shows why

At this unigue distance from isolation

It becomes still more difficult to find

Words at once true and kind,

Or not untrue and not unkind.

THOM GUNN

Considering the Snail

The snail pushes through a green

night, for the grass is heavy

with water and meets over

the bright path he makes, where rain

has darkened the earth's dark. He

这是两个人真心相待的标志。

但越来越多的时间无声过去。
外面的风并不大却吹个不止,
吹得空中的云有时散有时聚,

而地平线上是黑压压的城镇。
它们不关心我们。如此独特的
距离绝不会隔绝,但没什么表明:

为什么要找真挚又亲切的话——
或者并非不真挚不亲切的话——
现在已变得困难越来越增加。

冈恩 (1929—2004)

细看蜗牛

蜗牛推进在绿莹莹的
夜里,因为草上沾了水
重得交垂在它所造成
的亮晶晶路上,那儿雨
使大地的乌黑更乌黑。

moves in a wood of desire,

pale antlers barely stirring

as he hunts. I cannot tell

what power is at work, drenched there

with purpose, knowing nothing,

what is a snail's fury? All

I think is that if later

I parted the blades above

the tunnel and saw the thin

trail of broken white across

litter, I would never have

imagined the slow passion

to that deliberate progress.[1]

1　本诗诗节有固定韵式 abcabc, 但用来"押韵"的是诗行末尾的音，而不是诗行末尾的音节，且不以音步建行，而以音节建行（每行七个音节），重音的出现并无规律，既体现了对英诗诗律的探索，又别具一格，配合诗的内容，显示出蜗牛（及其他生物）在严酷环境中的奋斗。

它移动在欲望的林中，

苍白的触须在搜寻时
几乎不动。我不知什么
力量在驱动，全身湿透
在那里，有目的却不知
蜗牛的奋斗是什么？我
想到的只是，即便以后

我分开它那隧洞上的
草叶，看见满地狼藉上
它那一缕断续的白迹，
也永远不会想到它那
缓慢的激情同它那种
审慎的前进间的联系。

ROGER MCGOUGH

40—Love[1]

middle	aged
couple	playing
ten-	nis
when	the
game	ends
and	they
go	home
the	net
will	still
be	be-
tween	them

---

[1] 本诗内容为打网球，排列上也表明夫妇隔着球网一来一往打球，标题像是记分，"40—love"即 3 比 0，这里的 love 显然双关，这标题可解释为（中年夫妇）40 岁时的爱情。这双关很难译出，但汉语方块字用在这里更像网球，也更自然。这诗在另一版本中的排印另有特点，就是没有象征球网的中线，只有象征球场的矩形方框，而除了标题的所有文字，都贴着左右的"边线"排列。另外，本诗的译文与原作一样无韵，如果为了"美化"而在译文中用韵，似有违作者本意而有画蛇添足之嫌。

麦克高夫 (1937—)

40∶0

中年　夫妇
打着　网球
待　　到
打　　完
球　　回
家　　那
球　　网
仍　　将
隔　　在
他　　们
中　　间

SEAMUS HEANEY

The Forge[1]

All I know is a door into the dark.

Outside, old axles and iron hoops rusting;

Inside, the hammered anvil's short-pitched ring,

The unpredictable fantail of sparks

Or hiss when a new shoe toughens in water.

The anvil must be somewhere in the centre,

Horned as a unicorn, at one end square,

Set there immovable: an altar

Where he expends himself in shape and music.

Sometimes, leather-aproned, hairs in his nose,

He leans out on the jamb, recalls a clatter

Of hoofs where traffic is flashing in rows;

Then grunts and goes in, with a slam and flick

To beat real iron out, to work the bellows.

1　本诗是十四行诗，韵式为 abbaccddefcfef，但这里的用韵有现代特点，例如押相似韵，且不押在重读音节上。

希尼 (1939—2013)

打铁铺

我只知道是扇通向黑暗的门。
外面的旧轴和铁箍都在生锈;
里面铁砧上的锤声响得尖促,
还有无法预见的散射的火星
或者新马掌入水淬火的咝咝。
铁砧总放在中间的什么位置,
一头方,一头是独角兽似的角,
在这个固定的祭坛上他消耗
自己,消耗于定形和音乐声响。
围着皮作裙,鼻孔露鼻毛的他
有时倚着窗框朝外看,回忆着
如今车流闪闪处的蹄声嗒嗒;
接着他哼哼回里头拉起风箱,
为制作真正的铁器砰啪捶打。

PART THREE

American Poems

第 三 部 分

美国诗

CONTENTS

ANNE BRADSTREET The Author to Her Book

PHILIP FRENEAU The Volunteer's March

FRANCIS SCOTT KEY The Defense of Fort McHenry

WILLIAM CULLEN BRYANT To a Waterfowl

RALPH WALDO EMERSON Concord Hymn

NATHANIEL HAWTHORNE 'Oh Could I Raise the Darken'd Veil'

HENRY WADSWORTH LONGFELLOW A Psalm of Life

JOHN GREENLEAF WHITTIER In School-Days

EDGAR ALLAN POE Eldorado

OLIVER WENDELL HOLMES Old Ironside

HENRY DAVID THOREAU Nature

JAMES RUSSELL LOWELL Auf Wiedersehen

HERMAN MELVILLE The Night-March

WALT WHITMAN O Captain! My Captain!

JULIA WARD HOWE Battle Hymn of the Republic

FRANCES E. W. HARPER The Slave Auction

HENRY TIMROD 'I Know Not Why, But All This Weary Day'

EMILY DICKINSON 'There Is No Frigate Like a Book'

JOAQUIN MILLER Columbus

SIDNEY LANIER Struggle

EMMA LAZARUS The New Colossus

目录

安妮·布拉兹特里特 (1612—1672) 作者致自己的诗集

弗瑞诺 (1752—1832) 义勇军进行曲

克伊 (1779—1843) 保卫麦克亨利堡

布莱恩特 (1794—1878) 致水鸟

爱默生 (1803—1882) 康科德赞歌

霍桑 (1804—1864) "我若能掀起眼前的黑幕"

朗费罗 (1807—1882) 生之颂

惠蒂埃 (1807—1892) 做学童的日子里

坡 (1809—1849) 爱尔多拉多

霍姆斯 (1809—1894) 老铁甲

梭罗 (1817—1862) 大自然

洛威尔 (1819—1891) Auf Wiedersehen

梅尔维尔 (1819—1891) 夜行军

惠特曼 (1819—1892) 哦船长！我的船长！

朱莉娅·沃德·豪 (1819—1910) 共和国战歌

弗朗西丝·E. W. 哈帕 (1825—1911) 奴隶拍卖

蒂姆若德 (1828—1867) "不知为什么，整整这一天很丧气"

艾米莉·狄金森 (1830—1886) "没任何舰船能像一本书"

米勒 (1837—1913) 哥伦布

拉尼尔 (1842—1881) 拼搏

艾玛·拉扎勒斯 (1849—1887) 新的巨像

ELLA WHEELER WILCOX Solitude

EUGENE FIELD Little Boy Blue

EDWIN MARKHAM Outwitted

KATHARINE LEE BATES America the Beautiful

HARRIET MONROE Love Song

FRANK DEMPSTER SHERMAN A Quatrain

EDGAR LEE MASTERS 'When under the Icy Eaves'

EDWIN ARLINGTON ROBINSON The Dark Hills

JAMES WELDON JOHNSON My City

PAUL LAURENCE DUNBAR Harriet Beecher Stowe

ROBERT FROST The Road Not Taken

ADELAIDE CRAPSEY On Seeing Weather-Beaten Trees

WALLACE STEVENS Anecdote of the Jar

GEORGIA DOUGLAS JOHNSON 'I Want to Die While You Love Me'

JOHN GNEISENAU NEIHARDT 'Let Me Live Out My Years in Heat of Blood'

EDGAR A. GUEST It Can't Be Done

WILLIAM CARLOS WILLIAMS The Red Wheelbarrow

SARA TEASDALE Let It Be Forgotten

ELINOR WYLIE Let No Charitable Hope

EZRA POUND A Virginal

ALFRED JOYCE KILMER Tree

MARIANNE MOORE A Talisman

JOHN CROWE RANSOM Piazza Piece

埃拉·惠勒·威尔科克斯 (1850—1919) 孤独

菲尔德 (1850—1895) 蓝孩儿

马卡姆 (1852—1940) 棋高一着

凯瑟琳·李·贝茨 (1859—1929) 美丽的亚美利加

哈丽叶特·门罗 (1860—1936) 恋歌

舍尔曼 (1860—1916) 一首四行诗

马斯特斯 (1869—1950) "当结冰的檐下燕子来"

罗宾森 (1869—1935) 幽暗的山丘

J. W. 约翰逊 (1871—1938) 我的城市

邓巴 (1872—1906) 哈丽叶特·比彻·斯陀

弗罗斯特 (1874—1963) 没去走的路

阿德莱德·克莱普西 (1878—1914) 见饱经风雨的树有感

斯蒂文斯 (1879—1955) 坛子轶事

乔治娅·道格拉斯·约翰逊 (1880—1966) "我要在你爱我的时候死"

奈哈特 (1881—1973) "让我在热血沸腾中度此一生"

格斯特 (1881—1959) 这不可能完成

威廉斯 (1883—1963) 红颜色手推小车

萨拉·蒂斯代尔 (1884—1933) 让它被遗忘

埃莉诺·怀利 (1885—1928) 别让仁慈的希望

庞德 (1885—1972) 一架少女琴

基尔默 (1886—1918) 树

玛丽安娜·穆尔 (1887—1972) 一个护符

兰瑟姆 (1888—1974) 廊下曲

CONRAD AIKEN A Sonnet

CLAUDE MCKAY If We Must Die

EDNA ST. VINCENT MILLAY The Spring and the Fall

ROBERT PETER TRISTRAM COFFIN The Secret Heart

ARCHIBALD MACLEISH Immortal Autumn

E. E. CUMMINGS 'Me Up at Does'

ROSEMARY and STEPHEN BENÉT Western Wagons

MALCOLM COWLEY The Farm Died

ERNEST HEMINGWAY The Age Demanded

LANGSTON HUGHES Dreams

OGDEN NASH Love under the Republicans (or Democrats)

KENNETH REXROTH Song for a Dancer

WYSTAN HUGH AUDEN Song of the Master and Boatswain

THEODORE ROETHKE My Papa's Waltz

ELIZABETH BISHOP One Art

DUDLEY RANDALL The Melting Pot

GWENDOLYN BROOKS We Real Cool

HOWARD NEMEROV An Old Story

RICHARD WILBUR Candid

LOUIS SIMPSON To the Western World

WILLIAM BURFORD A Christmas Tree

艾肯 (1889—1973) 一首十四行诗

麦凯 (1890—1948) 如果我们必须死

爱德哪·圣文森特·米莱 (1892—1950) 春与秋

科芬 (1892—1955) 秘藏的心

麦克利什 (1892—1982) 不朽的秋

肯明斯 (1894—1962) "抬头盯视我"

勃耐夫妇 (1898—1943，1898—1962) 西行的大篷车

考利 (1898—1989) 死去的农庄

海明威 (1899—1961) 这时代曾要求

休斯 (1902—1967) 梦

纳什 (1902—1971) 共和党下的爱情(或民主党下的)

瑞克斯罗思 (1905—1982) 为一位舞者而唱

奥登 (1907—1973) 船长和水手长之歌

瑞特克 (1908—1963) 我爸爸的华尔兹

伊丽莎白·毕晓普 (1911—1979) 一种艺术

兰德尔 (1914—2000) 大熔炉

格温德琳·布鲁克斯 (1917—2000) 咱们真酷

内梅罗夫 (1920—1991) 一个老故事

威尔伯 (1921—2017) 率真

辛普森 (1923—2012) 致西方世界

伯福德 (1927—) 圣诞树

ANNE BRADSTREET

The Author to Her Book

Thou ill-formed offspring of my feeble brain,

Who after birth didst by my side remain,[1]

Till snatched from thence by friends, less wise than true,

Who thee abroad exposed to public view,

Made thee in rags, halting to th' press to trudge,[2]

Where errors were not lessened (all may judge).

At thy return my blushing was not small,

My rambling brat (in print) should mother call,

I cast thee by as one unfit for light,

Thy visage was so irksome in my sight;

Yet being mine own, at length affection would

Thy blemishes amend, if so I could:

I washed thy face, but more defects I saw,

And rubbing off a spot still made a flaw.

I stretched thy joints to make thee even feet,[3]

---

1 didst = did；-st 是从前加于动词的后缀，构成陈述语气第二人称单数，下面的 run'st, may'st, dost, hadst 同此。
2 th' = the，但这里不计音节，以符合格律。这情况在传统诗歌中常见。
3 feet 可意为英诗中的节奏单位音步。本诗音步主要由一轻一重两个音节构成，每行诗含五音步十音节，两行一韵，是当时流行的英雄双韵体（也称英雄偶句体，heroic couplet）。

安妮·布拉兹特里特 (1612—1672)

作者致自己的诗集

我虚弱的头脑生出难看的你；
出生后你本来同我待在一起，
直到被忠实的糊涂亲友拿掉，
把褴褛的你带了出去给人瞧，
让你瘸着腿费劲踏进印刷所：
人人看得出那里没帮你改错。
见你回来，我羞得涨红了面庞，
就怕白纸黑字的浑小鬼叫娘。
我把你丢开，感到你不该出生，
因为见你那模样我不免恼恨；
可毕竟是我骨肉，只要能做到，
我的爱总想使你的瑕疵减少：
我替你洗脸，却看见更多缺点；
擦去了污渍，还是留下个缺陷。
我拉你关节，要你双腿一样长，

Yet still thou run'st more hobbling than is meet;

In better dress to trim thee was my mind,

But nought save homespun cloth i' th' house I find.

In this array 'mongst vulgars may'st thou roam.

In critic's hands beware thou dost not come,

And take thy way where yet thou art not known;

If for thy father asked, say thou hadst none;

And for thy mother, she alas is poor,

Which caused her thus to send thee out of door.

PHILIP FRENEAU

The Volunteer's March[1]

Dulce Est pro Patria Mori.

Ye, whom Washington has led,

Ye, who in his footsteps tread,

Ye, who death nor danger dread,

 Haste to glorious victory.

---

1 本诗为鼓舞斗志之作，内容和格律都类似彭斯名作《苏格兰同袍》（见《英国名诗选》）。下一行是拉丁文名句，出自罗马诗人贺拉斯（公元前65—前8）代表作《歌集》第二卷。

可是一跑动,你跛得更不像样;
我想用漂亮衣裳把你打扮好,
但家里只能找到粗糙的布料。
穿这衣服去平民间流浪无妨,
可要留神别落进评论家手掌。
你去的地方要没人同你相熟,
要是谁问起你父亲,就说没有;
问起你母亲,就说她呀苦得很,
所以才让你这副模样出了门。

弗瑞诺 (1752—1832)

义勇军进行曲

为祖国而死就死得美

你们,一直是华盛顿部下,
你们,踩着他脚印跟着他,
你们,死亡和险阻都不怕,
　快争取光辉的胜利!

Now's the day and now's the hour;

See the British navy lour,

See approach proud George's power,[1]

    England! chains and slavery.

Who would be a traitor knave?

Who would fill a coward's grave?

Who so base to be a slave?

    Traitor, coward, turn and flee.

Meet the tyrants, one and all;

Freemen stand, or freemen fall —

At Columbia's patriot call,[2]

    At her mandate, march away!

Former times have seen them yield,

Seen them drove from every field,

Routed, ruin'd and repell'd —

    Seize the spirit of those times!

1　这里的 George 指当时的英国国王乔治三世。
2　Columbia 为美洲或美国的女性拟人化称呼，这女性穿红、白、蓝三色衣服。

今天的此刻要决定命运；
瞧不列颠舰队正在逼近，
瞧骄横的乔治正在进军——
　　英国是锁链和奴役！

谁愿做一个叛逆的贼子？
谁愿埋葬在懦夫坟墓里？
谁这么下贱宁愿做奴隶？
　　让他们快转身逃离！

要万众一心去迎战暴君；
死为自由鬼，生为自由人；
祖国母亲的呼唤是命令——
　　一听到就奋勇出击！

从前他们也多次打败仗，
被杀得逃离一处处战场，
只剩些溃散的残兵败将——
　　要抓住当时那精神！

By oppression's woes and pains —

By our sons in servile chains

We will bleed from all our veins

    But they shall be — shall be free.

O'er the standard of their power

Bid Columbia's eagle tower,

Give them hail in such a shower

    As shall blast them — horse and man!

Lay the proud invaders low,

Tyrants fall in every foe;

Liberty's in every blow,

    Forward! Let us do or die.

凭受压迫者的苦难起誓,
为子孙不受奴役而起誓,
我们愿流尽血管里的血,
　但他们必须获自由。

让哥伦比亚之鹰冲上天,
高高地在他们军旗上面;
我们要疾风暴雨般迎战——
　杀他们个人仰马翻!

杀败他们气汹汹的入侵;
死一个敌人,少一分暴政;
打击多一次,自由增一分,
　前进,不成功宁阵亡!

FRANCIS SCOTT KEY

The Defense of Fort McHenry[1]
(The Star-Spangled Banner)

O! say, can you see, by the dawn's early light
   What so proudly we hailed at the twilight's last gleaming.
Whose broad stripes and bright stars through the perilous fight,
   O'er the ramparts we watched were so gallantly streaming.
And the rockets' red glare, the bombs bursting in air,
Gave proof through the night that our flag was still there.
O! say, does that star-spangled banner yet wave
O'er the land of the free and the home of the brave?

On the shore, dimly seen through the mists of the deep,
   Where the foe's haughty host in dread silence reposes,
What is that which the breeze, o'er the towering steep,
   As it fitfully blows, half conceals, half discloses?

---

[1] 麦克亨利堡在马里兰州北部巴尔的摩港入口。1814年9月，英军火烧华盛顿后，克伊去切萨比克湾英军旗舰交涉，要求释放被当作间谍的医生朋友。舰队司令因仍在战斗，不愿立即让他们离开。他在船上被扣留一夜（13到14日），眼看英军猛轰麦克亨利堡而彻夜未眠。次晨他望见美国国旗仍飘扬在要塞上空，不禁在旧信封反面写下此诗，配以英国作曲家兼风琴师J. S. 史密斯（1750—1836）的祝酒歌《献给天国里的阿那克里翁》曲调，以传单形式流传并隐名发表于9月20日《巴尔的摩爱国者报》。后来此歌改名《星条旗》，风行全美，先后被陆、海军用为正式歌曲，1931年经国会通过，定为美国国歌。1939年该堡辟为纪念馆，成为历史胜地。

克伊 (1779—1843)

保卫麦克亨利堡

(星条旗)

你呀凭借着曙光能不能看见
　　夕照中让我们豪迈欢呼的旗?
激战中我们曾凝望壁垒上面,
　　那些星星和条条飘扬得壮丽!
炮弹发出的红光和空中爆炸
证明了我们的旗仍整夜高插。
那星条旗呀不照旧还在飘扬?——
飘扬在自由土地、勇士家园上!

海上的雾气里,海岸隐约可见,
　　骄敌歇在那里的可怕寂静中;
什么在那陡峭高处半隐半现——
　　当阵阵微风时不时把它吹动?

Now it catches the gleam of the morning's first beam,

In full glory reflected, now shines on the stream:

'Tis the star-spangled banner! Oh long may it wave

O'er the land of the free and the home of the brave!

And where is that band who so vauntingly swore

 That the havoc of war and the battle's confusion,

A home and a country should leave us no more?

 Their blood has washed out their foul footsteps' pollution.

No refuge could save the hireling and slave

From the terror of flight, or the gloom of the grave:

And the star-spangled banner in triumph doth wave[1]

O'er the land of the free and the home of the brave!

O! thus be it ever, when freemen shall stand

 Between their loved home and the war's desolation!

Blest with victory and peace, may the heav'n rescued land

 Praise the Power that hath made and preserved us a nation.

Then conquer we must, when our cause it is just,

And this be our motto: 'In God is our trust.'

And the star-spangled banner in triumph shall wave

O'er the land of the free and the home of the brave!

1　这面旗现保存于美国首都国家博物馆，约有一面墙大小，旗上有 11 个弹孔。

现在它接住第一道破晓初晖，
在阳光之中更闪出全部光辉。
这是星条旗！祝愿它永远飘扬——
飘扬在自由土地、勇士家园上！

敌人狂妄发誓说，厮杀的破坏
  和战争的浩劫，使我们再也不剩
家园和祖国；那帮人如今何在？
  他们的血洗掉了他们的脏脚印。
对于惊慌逃窜的雇佣兵和奴仆，
除了去坟墓，没地方能提供保护：
而星条旗将会胜利地招展飘扬——
飘扬在自由土地、勇士家园上！

哦！当自由人站在心爱的乡土
  和战争废墟间，愿这旗永远如此；
天佑的祖国受胜利与和平祝福，
  要颂赞使我们成为国家的伟力！
我们将必胜，当正义在我们一边；
"信赖上帝"便是我们的格言！
而星条旗将会胜利地招展飘扬——
飘扬在自由土地，勇士家园上！

WILLIAM CULLEN BRYANT

To a Waterfowl

  Whither, 'midst falling dew,
While glow the heavens with the last steps of day,
Far, through their rosy depths, dost thou pursue
  Thy solitary way?

  Vainly the fowler's eye
Might mark thy distant flight to do thee wrong,
As, darkly painted on the crimson sky,
  Thy figure floats along.

  Seek'st thou the plashy brink
Of weedy lake, or marge of river wide,
Or where the rocking billows rise and sink
  On the chafed ocean side?

  There is a Power whose care
Teaches thy way along that pathless coast, —
The desert and illimitable air, —
  Lone wandering, but not lost.

布莱恩特 (1794—1878)

致水鸟

　　眼下已在降露水，
行将结束的白昼使天空辉煌，
你在玫瑰红的深处孤独远飞——
　　你要去什么地方？

　　也许有猎鸟的人
看到你远飞，但是无法伤害你——
因为，满天的红霞衬着你身影，
　　只见你振翅飞去。

　　你想要飞往何处？
要寻觅杂草丛生的泥泞湖岸？
要寻找起伏海涛拍打的滩涂
　　或者江河的边沿？

　　在那无垠的长空，
在没有路径的海岸和沙漠上，
有神明关切地教你孤身前行——
　　飘零，却不会迷航。

All day thy wings have fanned
At that far height, the cold, thin atmosphere:
Yet stoop not, weary, to the welcome land,
  Though the dark night is near.

  And soon that toil shall end,
Soon shalt thou find a summer home, and rest,
And scream among thy fellows; reed shall bend,
  Soon, o'er thy sheltered nest.

  Thou'rt gone, the abyss of heaven
Hath swallowed up thy form; yet, on my heart
Deeply hath sunk the lesson thou hast given,
  And shall not soon depart.

  He, who, from zone to zone,
Guides through the boundless sky thy certain flight,
In the long way that I must tread alone,
  Will lead my steps aright.

你整天扑着翅膀，
扇着高空中冷冷的稀薄大气，
天快黑也不愿来惬意的地上，
　　尽管你已经乏力。
　　这辛苦不会久长；
你很快会找到一个歇夏的家
并随同伴欢叫；你荫里的窝上，
　　芦苇将把腰弯下。

　　你的形象已消失，
深邃的天吞没了你；但我心上，
你已经留下一个深刻的教益——
　　不会很快被遗忘。

　　谁教你南来北往，
指引你穿越长空的确定航路，
也会在我独自跋涉的长途上
　　正确引导我脚步。

RALPH WALDO EMERSON

Concord Hymn[1]

Sung at the Completion of the Battle Monument, July 4. 1837

By the rude bridge that arched the flood,
    Their flag to April's breeze unfurled,
Here once the embattled farmers stood
    And fired the shot heard round the world.

The foe long since in silence slept,
    Alike the conqueror silent sleeps;
And Time the ruined bridge has swept
    Down the dark stream which seaward creeps.

On this green bank, by this soft stream,
    We set today a votive stone;
That memory may their deed redeem,
    When, like our sires, our sons are gone.

---

1 Concord 在波士顿西北 92 公里,是爱默生出生地和住地,还住过霍桑等作家。1775 年 4 月 19 日,该地民兵向英军开枪,揭开独立战争序幕。1837 年 7 月 4 日,爱默生在该碑揭幕式上朗诵了被称为即兴诗杰作的本诗,后来其中第一节刻上该碑。

爱默生 (1803—1882)

康科德赞歌

为康科德之战纪念碑落成而咏
1837 年 7 月 4 日

当年在横跨河水的陋桥旁,
　　他们的旗帜在春风中招展;
这是庄稼汉战斗过的地方,
　　他们的枪声全世界都听见。

敌人早无声地长眠在地下,
　　胜利者也安安静静在沉睡;
毁坏的桥经不住时光冲刷,
　　落进了蜿蜒入海的黑河水。

在这道缓缓小河的绿岸上,
　　我们在今天立石碑表心愿:
尽管祖祖孙孙一代代消亡,
　　让先人的业绩仍被人怀念。

Spirit, that made those heroes dare

    To die, and leave their children free,

Bid Time and Nature gently spare

    The shaft we raise to them and thee.

NATHANIEL HAWTHORNE

'Oh Could I Raise the Darken'd Veil'

Oh could I raise the darken'd veil,

Which hides my future life from me,

Could unborn ages slowly sail,

Before my view—and could I see

My every action painted there,

To cast one look I would not dare.

There poverty and grief might stand,

And dark Despair's corroding hand,

Would make me seek the lonely tomb

To slumber in its endless gloom.

Then let me never cast a look,

Within Fate's fix'd mysterious book.

啊，曾激励英雄敢于牺牲，
　　勇于为子孙争自由的精神，
请吩咐时光和大自然留情——
　　让纪念他们和你的碑永存！

霍桑 (1804—1864)

"我若能掀起眼前的黑幕"

我若能掀起眼前的黑幕，
看到我将来的生活道路，
看到面前是未来的光阴
慢慢移过，而我所有言行
全清清楚楚地一一显现，
我也不敢朝那里看一眼。
那里可能有贫乏和悲愁，
还有绝望的侵蚀性黑手，
让我把凄清的坟墓寻觅，
去长眠在那无尽黑暗里。
所以，有定数的命运秘籍
让我的目光永远别触及。

HENRY WADSWORTH LONGFELLOW

A Psalm of Life[1]

Tell me not, in mournful numbers,
    Life is but an empty dream! —
For the soul is dead that slumbers,
    And things are not what they seem.[2]

Life is real! Life is earnest!
    And the grave is not its goal;
Dust thou art, to dust returnest,[3]
    Was not spoken of the soul.

Not enjoyment, and not sorrow,
    Is our destined end or way;
But to act, that each to-morrow
    Find us farther than to-day.

---

1 本诗的写作反映了作者正从消沉中振作起来,匿名发表后颇受好评,被称为"美国良知的心脏搏动声"和"行动时代的道德蒸汽机"。
2 本诗有很多格言式警句,其中心思想或文字往往来自前人著作,如此行内容出自罗马寓言家费德鲁斯(公元前15?—50?)。
3 据基督教的说法,上帝用泥土造人,死后仍归泥土。

朗费罗 (1807—1882)

生之颂

别对我唱那句悲切的诗,
　　说人生只是虚幻的梦!
因为灵魂的昏睡无异死,
　　而事物与其表象不同。

人生多真切! 它决非虚度!
　　它的归宿并不是丘坟;
你本是尘土,须归于尘土,
　　这话所指的不是灵魂。

我们命定的道路和终点
　　不是享乐也不是悲苦;
是行动:要让每一个明天
　　比今天都有新的进步。

Art is long, and Time is fleeting,[1]
  And our hearts, though stout and brave,
Still, like muffled drums, are beating
  Funeral marches to the grave.[2]

In the world's broad field of battle,
  In the bivouac of Life,
Be not like dumb, driven cattle!
  Be a hero in the strife!

Trust no Future, howe'er pleasant!
  Let the dead Past bury its dead![3]
Act, — act in the living Present!
  Heart within, and God o'erhead!

---

1 同样意思的话最早见于希腊几何学家希波克拉底（活动于公元前 460 年前后）著作。后来罗马作家塞内加、英诗之父乔叟、德国诗人歌德等人作品中都有类似语句。

2 军人葬礼中常以织物蒙鼓，使鼓声低沉。英国剧作家鲍蒙特（1584—1616）和弗莱彻（1579—1625）作品中有语：我们的生命只是向坟墓的行进过程。这两行受法国诗人波德莱尔（1821—1867）激赏，几乎原封不动移进其法语诗中。

3 《新约全书·马太福音》8 章 22 节："耶稣说，任凭死人埋葬他们的死人，你们跟从我吧。"

学艺费光阴，时日去匆促，
　　任我们的心勇敢坚强，
依然像那些蒙住的鼙鼓——
　　敲打着哀乐走向坟场。

在这个世界的广阔战场，
　　在这人生的野营帐篷，
别像被驱赶的沉默牛羊！
　　要做能征惯战的英雄！

将来再美好也别空企盼！
　　让死往昔把死的埋葬！
干！在活生生的现在就干！
　　胸中怀赤心，神明在上！

Lives of great men all remind us
　　We can make our lives sublime,
And, departing, leave behind us
　　Footprints on the sands of time;

Footprints, that perhaps another,
　　Sailing o'er life's solemn main,
A forlorn and shipwrecked brother,
　　Seeing, shall take heart again.

Let us, then, be up and doing,
　　With a heart for any fate;[1]
Still achieving, still pursuing,
　　Learn to labor and to wait.

1　拜伦的《致托马斯·穆尔》第 8 行为：Here's a heart for every fate。

伟人的生平向我们指明,
　　我们能够让此生高尚——
一旦离去后,我们的脚印
　　将会留在时间沙滩上。

在庄严的生活之海远航,
　　也许有兄弟遭到不幸——
他虽因航船沉没而绝望,
　　见那脚印却恢复信心。

让我们挺起身,行动起来,
　　去不断收获,不断追求;
凭对付任何命运的心怀,
　　去学会苦干,学会等候。

JOHN GREENLEAF WHITTIER

In School-Days[1]

Still sits the school-house by the road,
    A ragged beggar sleeping;
Around it still the sumachs grow,
    And blackberry-vines are creeping.

Within, the master's desk is seen,
    Deep scarred by rape official;
The warping floor, the battered seats,
    The jack-knife's carved initial;

The charcoal frescos in its wall;
    Its door's worn sill, betraying
The feet that, creeping slow to school,
    Went storming out to playing!

Long years ago a winter sun
    Shone over it at setting;
Lit up its western window-panes,
    And low eaves' icy fretting.

---

1 当年美国诗人霍姆斯读了本诗，曾对作者说，"以在学少年为题材的英语诗歌中，你写下了最美的一首。"

惠蒂埃 (1807—1892)

做学童的日子里

那学校的房子仍在路旁,
　像褴褛乞丐在睡眠;
它四周仍然有漆树围绕,
　有黑莓藤蔓在攀援。
看得见里面老师的桌子
　有几处被教鞭敲瘪;
翘起的地板,砸坏的座位,
　折刀刻的姓名缩写;

墙上是木炭涂成的壁画;
　磨损的门槛传消息:
来校时磨磨蹭蹭的腿脚
　出去玩就猛冲一气!

多年前的一天,冬日太阳
　落山的时候照耀它;
照亮它西面块块玻璃窗
　和低低檐上的冰花。

It touched the tangled golden curls,
　　And brown eyes full of grieving,
Of one who still her steps delayed
　　When all the school were leaving.

For near her stood the little boy
　　Her childish favor singled:
His cap pulled low upon a face
　　Where pride and shame were mingled.

Pushing with restless feet the snow
　　To right and left, he lingered;—
As restlessly her tiny hands
　　The blue-checked apron fingered.
He saw her lift her eyes; he felt
　　The soft hand's light caressing,
And heard the tremble of her voice,
　　As if a fault confessing.

'I'm sorry that I spelt the word:
　　I hate to go above you,
Because,'—the brown eyes lower fell,—
　　'Because, you see, I love you!'

夕阳照着纷乱的金鬈发，
　　棕色眼睛里是忧愁；
学校里的人全都在离去，
　　这姑娘却迟迟没走。

因为近旁站着的小男孩
　　独受她天真的钟爱；
男孩的神色自尊又羞愧，
　　拉低了帽舌把脸盖。

他也没有走，不安分的脚
　　把积雪往左右拨动；
姑娘的小手同样也不安——
　　把蓝格子围裙捏弄。
男孩感觉到纤手的轻抚，
　　看见她抬起了眼睛，
听到她说话的颤抖声音——
　　似乎在承认她罪行。

"我为拼出那个字而难过，
　　我最恨自己超过你，
因为，"她垂下棕色眼睛说，
　　"因为，要知道我爱你！"

Still memory to a gray-haired man
   That sweet child-face is showing.
Dear girl! The grasses on her grave
   Have forty years been growing!

He lives to learn, in life's hard school,
   How few who pass above him
Lament their triumph and his loss,
   Like her,—because they love him.

EDGAR ALLAN POE

Eldorado[1]

Gaily bedight,
A gallant knight,
In sunshine and in shadow,
Had journeyed long,
Singing a song,

---

[1] Eldorado 也作 El Dorado，来自西班牙语，原意为镀金人，是传说中波哥大附近一印第安统治者。据说每逢节日，他全身抹金粉，仪式后在湖中洗去，臣民则将金银珍宝投入湖中。后来 Eldorado 被说成是黄金国。早期西班牙殖民者在美洲寻找这传闻之地。作者在本诗中可能用以喻某种理想，某种难以达到目的的艺术追求或境界。

白发苍苍的老人还记得
  那张可爱的孩子脸。
亲爱的姑娘!她墓上的草
  至今已长了四十年!

在严峻的人生学校他得知:
  爱他、超过他的人中,
很少人能像那姑娘一样,
  竟为胜过他而悲痛。

坡 (1809—1849)

爱尔多拉多

  豪侠的骑士,
    华美的服饰,
任阳光似火夜如墨,
    他长途跋涉,
    他引吭高歌,

In search of Eldorado.

But he grew old —
This knight so bold —
And o'er his heart a shadow
Fell as he found
No spot of ground
That looked like Eldorado.

And, as his strength
Failed him at length,
He met a pilgrim shadow —
'Shadow,' said he,
'Where can it be —
This land of Eldorado?'
'Over the Mountains
Of the Moon,
Down the Valley of the Shadow,
Ride, boldly ride,'
The shade replied —
'If you seek for Eldorado!'

要寻找爱尔多拉多。

  他虽是英豪,
   却变得衰老,
阴影在他的心头落,
  因为他发现,
   没一个地点
看来像爱尔多拉多。

  到了临了时,
   他力竭精疲,
遇见个游荡的魂魄:
  "幽魂,"他讲,
   "在什么地方——
有这个爱尔多拉多?"
  "翻过月亮中
   一座座山峰,
走下阴影中的幽壑,
  驱马大胆找,"
   幽魂回答道,
"若要找爱尔多拉多。"

OLIVER WENDELL HOLMES

Old Ironside[1]

Ay, tear her tattered ensign down!
    Long has it waved on high,
And many an eye has danced to see
    That banner in the sky;
Beneath it rung the battle shout,
    And burst the cannon's roar; —
The meteor of the ocean air
    Shall sweep the clouds no more!

Her deck, once red with heroes' blood,
    Where knelt the vanquished foe,
When winds were hurrying o'er the flood,
    And waves were white below,
No more shall feel the victor's tread,
    Or know the conquered knee; —
The harpies of the shore shall pluck

---

1 Ironside 本是英王爱德蒙（981—1016）的外号，17 世纪革命时保王党人用来称呼清教徒派领袖克伦威尔。1644 年 7 月，他的骑兵大败保王军，这称呼也用于这支军队，含"坚韧、勇敢、果断者"或"铁人""铁军"意，现用来称装甲战舰。这在本诗指战舰"宪法号"，这是美国海军第一批驱逐舰之一，1797 年在波士顿下水，1812 年参加反英战争，立下战功。1828 年准备拆毁，但本诗起了保护作用，1927—1931 年修复后停泊在波士顿展览。本舰虽称"老铁甲"，但并未装甲，因为军舰装甲始于十九世纪中期。

霍姆斯 (1809—1894)

老铁甲

嗨,去撕下她那面破舰旗!
　　它久久在高处飘扬;
多少只眼睛曾转来转去,
　　把空中这舰旗仰望;
旗下曾是战斗的厮杀声,
　　是炮火连天的呼啸;
但这飘在大洋上空的旗
　　再不会把云霞驱扫!

当初海面上猛刮着疾风,
　　舰下是白色的波涛;
英雄的血染红的甲板上,
　　战败的敌人曾跪倒;
甲板再感不到胜者脚步,
　　也不知败者的屈膝——
岸上有一些狠毒的怪物

The eagle of the sea!

O, better that her shattered hulk
 Should sink beneath the wave;
Her thunders shook the mighty deep,
 And there should be her grave;
Nail to the mast her holy flag,
 Set every threadbare sail,
And give her to the god of storms,
 The lightning and the gale!

HENRY DAVID THOREAU

Nature

O nature! I do not aspire

To be the highest in thy choir, —

To be a meteor in the sky,

Or comet that may range on high;

Only a zephyr that may blow

Among the reeds by the river low;

Give me thy most privy place

Where to run my airy race.

要拔这海鹰的毛羽!

啊,这船体已遭受过重创,
 最好是沉她到海底;
她的轰击曾震撼过大海,
 她的墓就该在那里;
把她神圣的旗钉上桅杆,
 张开她每一张旧帆,
把她奉献给风暴的神明,
 奉献给狂飙和雷电!

梭罗 (1817—1862)

大自然

哦,大自然!我并不渴求
做你唱诗班的最高歌手
或是做空中的一颗流星
或是做彗星在太空运行;
我只求做一阵轻拂的风
吹在浅浅河边的芦苇中;
请给我最最隐秘的地方,
让我在空中驰骋得欢畅。

In some withdrawn unpublic mead

Let me sigh upon a reed,

Or in the woods, with leafy din,

Whisper the still evening in:

Some still work give me to do, —

Only — be it near to you!

For I had rather be thy child

And pupil, in the forest wild,

Than be the king of men elsewhere,

And most sovereign slave of care;

To have one moment of thy dawn

Than share the city's year forlorn.

JAMES RUSSELL LOWELL

Auf Wiedersehen[1]

Sum mer

The little gate was reached at last,

    Half hid in lilacs down the lane;

---

1 德语：意为"再见"，读作 [auf'viːdərzeːən]，用于各诗节末行，也与各节第二行押韵。

在人所不知的偏僻草地，
让我对一株芦苇发叹息，
或在叶片沙沙响的树林
咕哝着迎来安恬的黄昏：
请把安恬的活儿给我干——
只希望同你距离近一点！

因为我宁可在莽莽林中
做你的孩子和你的学童，
也不去别处做人间皇帝，
去成为烦恼的至尊奴隶；
享有你黎明的片刻光阴
胜过城市里一年的伶仃。

洛威尔 (1819—1891)

Auf Wiedersehen

夏

终于走到了巷子那一头
　半掩在紫丁香中的小门；

She pushed it wide, and, as she past,
A wistful look she backward cast,
 And said, — *'Auf wiedersehen!'*

With hand on latch, a vision white
 Lingered reluctant, and again
Half doubting if she did aright,
Soft as the dews that fell that night,
 She said, — *'Auf wiedersehen!'*

The lamp's clear gleam flits up the stair;
 I linger in delicious pain;
Ah, in that chamber, whose rich air
To breathe in thought I scarcely dare,
 Thinks she, — *'Auf wiedersehen?'* ...

'Tis thirteen years; once more I press[1]
 The turf that silences the lane;
I hear the rustle of her dress,
I smell the lilacs, and — ah, yes,

---

[1] 诗人的妻子玛丽亚·怀特（生于 1821 年）也写诗，是著名的废奴主义者，对丈夫的影响很大。本诗发表于 1854 年。她去世于 1853 年 10 月，距离她和诗人订婚的 1840 年（结婚于 1844 年）正好十三年。

推开门,正在进去的时候,
她带着依依的神情回眸,
　　　说了声 Auf wiedersehen！

手搭着门销,她欲去还留,
　　这白色人影似乎在自忖:
这样是不是有点不对头?
话语声像那晚露水轻柔,
　　　她是说 Auf wiedersehen！

灯盏的清光掠上了楼梯,
　　我却流连在甜蜜痛苦中,
啊,那房间里馥郁的空气
我都不敢在想象中呼吸——
　　　她会想 Auf wiedersehen？……

十三年过去,我重来此处,
　　这草地让巷子寂静无声;
我仍听见她衣裙的窸窣;
仍闻到紫丁香,哦,还有——

I hear *'Auf wiedersehen!'*

Sweet piece of bashful maiden art!
　　The English words had seemed too fain,
But these — they drew us heart to heart,
Yet held us tenderly apart;
　　She said, *'Auf wiedersehen!'*

HERMAN MELVILLE

The Night-March

With banners furled, the clarions mute,
　　An Army passes in the night,
And beaming spears and helms salute
　　The dark with bright.

In silence deep the legions stream,
　　With open ranks, in order true;
Over boundless plains they stream and gleam —
　　No chief in view!

Afar, in twinkling distance lost,

我听见 Auf wiedersehen！

腼腆姑娘那可爱的心计！
　说那英语词似乎太热心，
而这把两颗心牵在一起，
却又让我们仍隔点距离——
　她说了 Auf wiedersehen！

梅尔维尔 (1819—1891)

夜行军

号角不鸣，战旗紧卷，
　一支部队在夜里行军；
矛尖和头盔银光点点——
　向黑暗致敬。

队列散开，秩序井然，
　军团肃静地向前涌动；
平原无垠，大军隐现，
　却不见元戎！

远处微光闪闪，据说，

(So legends tell) he lonely wends

And back through all that shining host

His mandate sends.

WALT WHITMAN

O Captain! My Captain![1]

O Captain! my Captain! our fearful trip is done,

The ship has weathered every rack, the prize we sought is won,

The port is near, the bells I hear, the people all exulting,

While follow eyes the steady keel, the vessel grim and daring;

But O heart! heart! heart!

O the bleeding drops of red,

Where on the deck my captain lies,

Fallen cold and dead.

O Captain! my Captain! rise up and hear the bells;

Rise up — for you the flag is flung — for you the bugle trills,

For you bouquets and ribboned wreaths — for you the shores acrowding,

---

[1] 1865年，林肯领导下的北方刚战胜南方便遇刺身亡。这里"船长"喻林肯，"船"喻林肯领导的国家。惠特曼突破格律，是写自由诗的旗手，但本诗显然有格律，形式感非常突出。

他独自走得无踪无影,

后面的队伍寒光闪烁——

  传遍他号令。

惠特曼 (1819—1892)

哦船长！我的船长！

哦船长！我的船长！我们可怕的航行已终了,

船历经种种艰险,我们追求的锦标已夺到；

港口已很近,钟声已听到,人们都欢欣鼓舞,

眼睛都盯着破浪前进的船,她威严而勇武；

   但心哪！心哪！心哪！

    哦,滴滴的血在淌；

     我的船长倒在这甲板上,

      冰凉地已经死亡。

哦船长！我的船长！起来听听这一片钟声吧；

起来吧！为了你,人们升了旗,吹起激越的喇叭,

备了花束、飘缎带的花环；为了你,人挤满海岸,

For you they call, the swaying mass, their eager faces turning;
    Here Captain! dear father!
        The arm beneath your head!
           It is some dream that on the deck,
              You've fallen cold and dead.

My Captain does not answer, his lips are pale and still,
My father does not feel my arm, he has no pulse nor will,
The ship is anchored safe and sound, its voyage closed and done,
From fearful trip the victor ship comes in with object won:
    Exult O shores, and ring O bells!
        But I with mournful tread,
           Walk the deck my Captain lies,
              Fallen cold and dead.

JULIA WARD HOWE

Battle Hymn of the Republic[1]

Mine eyes have seen the glory of the coming of the Lord;

---

1 本诗是南北战争期间流行于北军的歌曲。作者1861年访问北军,有感于士兵歌唱流行的进步歌曲《约翰·布朗的遗体》,按其曲调写下此诗,1862年发表于著名的《大西洋月刊》(稿酬四美元)后,备受欢迎并流行至今。

为了你，人群涌动着，转过殷切的脸在呼喊；
　　可船长啊！亲爱的父亲！
　　　你的头搁在这臂膀上！
　　　　这是梦，你倒在这甲板上，
　　　　　冰凉地已经死亡。

我的船长不回答，他苍白的嘴唇没发出声响；
我父亲感觉不到这臂膀，他没有脉息和愿望；
船已经安安稳稳地下了锚，她的航程已终了；
可怕的航行后，胜利的船归来，目标已达到；
　　狂欢吧，海岸！敲吧，钟！
　　　可是我满怀着哀伤，
　　　　走在船长倒下的甲板，
　　　　　他冰凉地已经死亡。

朱莉娅·沃德·豪 (1819—1910)

共和国战歌

我的眼睛看见过主耶稣来临时那种光灿：

He is trampling out the vintage where the grapes of wrath are stored;[1]

He hath loosed the fateful lightning of his terrible swift sword;

  His truth is marching on.

I have seen him in the watch-fires of a hundred circling camps;

They have builded him an altar in the evening dews and damps;

I have read his righteous sentence by the dim and flaring lamps;

  His day is marching on.

I have read a fiery gospel, writ in burnished rows of steel;

'As ye deal with my contemners, so with you my grace shall deal;

Let the Hero, born of woman, crush the serpent with his heel,[2]

  Since God is marching on.'

He has sounded forth his trumpet that shall never call retreat;

He is sifting out the hearts of men before His judgment-seat;

O be swift, my soul, to answer him! be jubilant, my feet!

  Our God is marching on.

In the beauty of the lilies Christ was born, across the sea,

1　grapes of wrath 语出《新约全书·启示录》14 章 19、20 节，意为骚动不宁的根源或愤慨暴乱的种子。

2　可参阅《旧约全书·创世纪》3 章 15 节。

他正在贮藏"愤怒葡萄"的地方把它们踩烂；
他抽出可怕的迅猛之剑，发出致命的闪电：
　　他的真理在行进。

我看见过他，见他在一百座团团军营营火里；
在傍晚露水和潮气里，他们为他把圣坛建立；
我凭着忽暗忽亮的灯光，阅读他正义的词句：
　　他的时代在行进。

我读过一行行用擦亮的钢写成的火样福音；
"我是否恩典你，要看你如何对待藐视我的人；
让女子生养的英雄把那条毒蛇踩死在脚跟，
　　因为上帝在行进。"

他响亮吹起的喇叭永远也不会叫人后撤；
在他的审判座前，他在把人们的心筛分着：
我的灵魂哪快快答复他！我的脚呀该欢乐！
　　我们的上帝在行进。

在大海那边，基督降生在百合花的美丽中，

With a glory in his bosom that transfigures you and me;
As he died to make men holy, let us die to make men free!
　　While God is marching on.

FRANCES E. W. HARPER

The Slave Auction

The sale began — young girls were there,
　Defenseless in their wretchedness,
Whose stifled sobs of deep despair
　Revealed their anguish and distress.

And mothers stood with streaming eyes,
　And saw their dearest children sold;
Unheeded rose their bitter cries,
　While tyrants bartered them for gold.

And woman, with her love and truth —
　For these in sable forms may dwell —
Gazed on the husband of her youth,
　With anguish none may paint or tell.

他胸中的荣耀使你和我变得与从前不同；

他为让人圣洁而死，我们要为解放人而终，

　　　因为上帝在行进。

弗朗西丝·E. W. 哈帕 (1825—1911)

奴隶拍卖

拍卖了。那些年轻的姑娘
　　命运既悲惨又全然无助；
强忍着的抽泣出自绝望，
　　显示出她们悲伤和痛苦。

母亲们站在那里泪涟涟，
　　眼看心爱的孩子像货物——
硬是被恶霸卖了换银钱，
　　根本不理会做娘的痛哭。

深褐色胸中同样有情愫——
　　女奴满怀着忠诚和挚爱，
凝视着她年轻时的丈夫；
　　却没人能描述她的悲哀。

And men, whose sole crime was their hue,

    The impress of their Maker's hand,

And frail and shrinking children, too,

    Were gathered in that mournful band.

Ye who have laid your love to rest,

    And wept above their lifeless clay,

Know not the anguish of that breast,

    Whose lov'd are rudely torn away.

Ye may not know how desolate

    Are bosoms rudely forced to part,

And how a dull and heavy weight

    Will press the life-drops from the heart.

HENRY TIMROD

'I Know Not Why, But All This Weary Day'

I know not why, but all this weary day,

Suggested by no definite grief or pain,

Sad fancies have been flitting through my brain;

Now it has been a vessel losing way,

男奴和瘦弱畏缩的孩子
　　也给赶进那哀哀的一群；
他们唯一的罪状是肤色——
　　可那是造物主留的手印。

你们哪曾给亲人送过殡，
　　曾在他们遗体上流过泪，
亲人硬给拽走时的伤心
　　你们却似乎并不能体会！

你们怎知道，硬被拆散的
　　亲人们心中是多么凄惨！
沉重的压力又将怎样地
　　把心头那生命之血榨干。

蒂姆若德 (1828—1867)

"不知为什么，整整这一天很丧气"

不知为什么，整整这一天很丧气，
尽管并没有具体的痛苦或忧伤，
脑海中却总是掠过可悲的幻想；
忽而是暴风雨交加的海角岬地，

Rounding a stormy headland; now a grey

Dull waste of clouds above a wintry main;

And then, a banner, drooping in the rain,

And meadows beaten into bloody clay.

Strolling at random with this shadowy woe

At heart, I chanced to wander hither! Lo!

A league of desolate marsh-land, with its lush,

Hot grasses in a noisome, tide-left bed,

And faint, warm airs, that rustle in the hush,

Like whispers round the body of the dead![1]

EMILY DICKINSON

'There Is No Frigate Like a Book'

There is no frigate like a book

To take us lands away,

Nor any coursers like a page

Of prancing poetry:

This traverse may the poorest take

Without oppress of toll;

---

1 这首十四行诗韵式较特别，前八行为典型的意大利式 abbaabba，后六行为 ccdede。

有一艘迷航的船正在绕过那里；
忽而是乌云笼罩的寒飕飕海洋；
接着是军旗耷拉在雨中的景象，
是被击打成血淋淋泥土的草地。
我信步而走，心中是莫名的苦恼，
说也巧，却正在走向那地方！瞧！
一大片荒凉的沼泽地，臭味熏人，
满是热烘烘的繁草，潮水已退去，
无力的暖风在寂静中瑟瑟作声，
像死者遗体周围那低声的话语。

艾米莉·狄金森 (1830—1886)

"没任何舰船能像一本书"

没任何舰船能像一本书
载我们行驶去异乡，
也没有骏马能像一页诗
载我们奔驰向远方。
这样的旅行穷人能负担，
还不必缴纳通行税；

How frugal is the chariot

That bears the human soul!

JOAQUIN MILLER

Columbus[1]

Behind him lay the gray Azores,[2]

 Behind the Gates of Hercules;[3]

Before him not the ghost of shores,

 Before him only shoreless seas.

The good mate said: 'Now must we pray,

 For lo! the very stars are gone.

Brave Admiral, speak, what shall I say?'

 'Why, say, "Sail on! sail on! and on!"'

---

1 Columbus (1451—1506) 因富于理想和冒险精神,发现了欧洲人眼中的新大陆(但他以为是印度附近岛屿)成为最伟大的航海家之一。他出生于寄居热那亚的西班牙犹太织布工家庭,14 岁开始海上生活,当过海盗。他向西航行到印度的计划被西班牙接受后,得到舰队司令名义和百万金币装备,于 1492 年 8 月出发。

2 Azores 指大西洋北部的亚速尔群岛。

3 Gates of Hercules 指直布罗陀。根据神话,直布罗陀海峡两岸的巨大岩石原是相连的,后被大力神 Hercules 分开,故又称海格利斯之柱。

这供人心灵搭乘的轻车

能俭省多少的花费!

米勒 (1837—1913)

哥伦布

他后面是灰濛濛的亚速尔,

 海格立斯之门更远在后面;

他前面没一点海岸的影子,

 他前面只有不见岸的海面。

好大副说:"现在我们得祈祷,

 因为天上已不见了那些星。

勇敢的司令,要我说什么好?"

 "就说'航行!继续航行!'"

'My men grow mutinous day by day;
  My men grow ghastly wan and weak.'
The stout mate thought of home; a spray
  Of salt wave washed his swarthy cheek.
'What shall I say, brave Admiral, say,
  If we sight naught but seas at dawn?'
'Why, you shall say at break of day,
  "Sail on! sail on! sail on! and on!"'

They sailed and sailed, as winds might blow,
  Until at last the blanched mate said:
'Why, now not even God would know
  Should I and all my men fall dead.
These very winds forget their way,
  For God from these dread seas is gone.
Now speak, brave Admiral, speak and say'—
  He said: 'Sail on! sail on! and on!'

They sailed. They sailed. Then spoke the mate:
  'This mad sea shows his teeth to-night,
He curls his lip, he lies in wait,
  With lifted teeth, as if to bite!
Brave Admiral, say but one good word:

"船员一天天已变得敢反抗；
　　已苍白虚弱得叫人见了怕。"
强壮的大副想着家；一个浪
　　把海水洒满他黝黑的脸颊。
"天明时，海上若啥也看不到，
　　勇敢的司令，我该传什么令？"
"我看，破晓时你就得说道：
　　'继续航行！继续航行！'"

他们任风刮，航行再航行，
　　面如土色的大副忍不住道：
"唉，现在连上帝也说不清
　　全船人的性命会不会送掉。
上帝已把这可怕的海撒下，
　　所以这些风胡乱地吹不停。
勇敢的司令，你现在请发话。"——
　　他说："航行！继续航行！"

航行再航行，大副又开口：
　　"这怒海狂涛今晚露出牙，
它噘起嘴，在埋伏中守候，
　　张开的牙床似乎快咬下！
既毫无希望，我们该怎么干？

What shall we do when hope is gone?'
The words leapt like a leaping sword:
'Sail on! sail on! sail on! and on!'

Then, pale and worn, he kept his deck,
And peered through darkness. Ah, that night
Of all dark nights! And then a speck—
A light! A light! A light! A light!
It grew, a starlit flag unfurled!
It grew to be Time's burst of dawn.[1]
He gained a world; he gave that world
Its grandest lesson: 'On! sail on!'[2]

SIDNEY LANIER

Struggle

My soul is like the oar that momently
Dies in a desperate stress beneath the wave,
Then glitters out again and sweeps the sea:
Each second I'm new born from some new grave.

---

1 有的历史学家把哥伦布发现新大陆的 1492 年作为中世纪和近代的分界线。
2 本诗是米勒最著名的作品，最后这短句曾是美国数百万小学生的口头语。

勇敢的司令，下个好命令。"
他说出的话像出鞘的剑：
　"继续航行！继续航行！"

于是憔悴的他守着甲板，
　透过最浓重的夜色了望。
那一夜！终于看到光一点——
　是火光，火光！是火光，火光！
火光大起来，扬起星星旗！
　随后化成新时代的黎明。
他赢得个世界，给这世界
　最豪迈的教诲："继续航行！"

拉尼尔 (1842—1881)

拼搏

我的灵魂就像桨，在波涛之下
　因为死命的奋力，而短暂殒灭，
接着又闪烁而出，在海上一划：
　每秒钟，新生的我跳出新墓穴。

EMMA LAZARUS

The New Colossus[1]

Not like the brazen giant of Greek fame
   With conquering limbs astride from land to land;[2]
   Here at our sea-washed, sunset gates shall stand
A mighty woman with a torch, whose flame
Is the imprisoned lightning, and her name
   Mother of Exiles. From her beacon-hand
   Glows world-wide welcome, her mild eyes command
The air-bridged harbor that twin cities frame.[3]

1　指纽约港内自由神岛（也叫贝德罗岛）上的自由女神像，正式名称为"自由照耀世界之神"。像高约45米，连基座92米。美国南北战争后法国史家建议，由法国人民捐款，法国雕塑家主持并由后来建造巴黎铁塔的埃菲尔工程师设计像中骨架，1885年这一纪念法、美人民友谊的巨像完成，运到纽约后建起基座并安装，1886年10月28日揭幕。

2　指古代世界七大奇观之一的青铜巨像，在爱琴海最东部的罗得岛，为纪念该岛解除德米特里的长期围困（公元前305—前304）而建在该岛港口。像高三十多米，是太阳神赫利俄斯的形象。建像费时12年（公元前292—前280），但几十年后毁于地震。据说该像双脚踏在航道两侧岸上，船只在像的胯下通过。

3　新泽西州的东北部城市泽西位于哈德孙河和哈肯萨克河之间的半岛上，与纽约的曼哈顿岛相望。

艾玛·拉扎勒斯 (1849—1887)

新的巨像

不像希腊那著名的巨大铜像
  以征服者的双脚跨两岸土地:
  这里要有擎火炬的伟大妇女
站在我们浪拍夕阳照的门旁。
她叫去国者之母,那火炬之光
  是握中闪电。她握炬之手闪示
  遍及世界的欢迎,她柔眼俯视
以水天相连的双城构成海港。

'Keep, ancient lands, your storied pomp!' Cries she,
  With silent lips, 'Give me your tired, your poor,
Your huddled masses yearning to breathe free,
  The wretched refuse of your teeming shore,
Send these, the homeless, tempest-tost to me,
  I lift my lamp beside the golden door!'

ELLA WHEELER WILCOX

Solitude

Laugh and the world laughs with you;
  Weep, and you weep alone;
For this brave old earth must borrow its mirth,
  It has trouble enough of its own.
Sing, and the hills will answer;
  Sigh! It is lost on the air;
The echoes bound to a joyful sound,
  But shrink from voicing care.

Rejoice, and men will seek you;
  Grieve, and they turn and go;
They want full measure of all your pleasure,

"古老大陆,留着你有名的奢华,
　你那里太拥挤!"她在无声呼喊,
"把你土地上疲惫的不幸'人渣',
　把渴望自由呼吸的贫妇穷汉,
把风吹雨打的无家者给我吧!
　我举着明灯站在这金色门边!"

埃拉·惠勒·威尔科克斯 (1850—1919)

孤独

你欢笑,人们就同你一起笑;
　你流泪,却独自流泪;
这华美老世界,欢乐就靠借;
　它自己的麻烦已成堆。
你歌唱,山丘会应和;
　你叹息,会被风吹走——
回声总蹦向快活的声响,
　但听到哀诉就退后。

你高兴,人家就来亲近你;
　你伤心,他们转身走——
人家要你的全部的喜乐,

But they do not want your woe.
Be glad, and your friends are many;
 Be sad, and you lose them all —
There are none to decline your nectared wine,
 But alone you must drink life's gall.

Feast, and your halls are crowded;
 Fast, and the world goes by,
Succeed and give, and it helps you live,
 But no man can help you die.
There is room in the halls of pleasure
 For a long and lordly train:
But one by one we must all file on[1]
 Through the narrow aisles of pain.

EUGENE FIELD

Little Boy Blue

The little toy dog is covered with dust,
 But sturdy and staunch he stands;

1　本诗各节的第三和第七行无尾韵，但有行中韵。这行的 one 与 on 也是。

但是不需要你的愁。
你欢快，朋友就很多；
　　你悲哀，他们全跑光——
没人会拒绝你琼浆玉液，
　　但生活苦汁你独尝。

你设宴，大厅就挤满宾客；
　　你斋戒，没人来拜访。
成功又慷慨，日子就愉快；
　　你要死，可没人帮忙。
喜气洋厅堂容得下
　　气宇轩昂的长队伍；
但是痛苦的狭窄侧廊里，
　　我们得一一挨过去。

菲尔德 (1850—1895)

蓝孩儿

小小的玩具狗满身是灰，
　　仍雄赳赳傲然肃立；

The little toy soldier is red with rust,
    And his musket moulds in his hands.
Time was when the little toy dog was new,
    And the soldier was passing fair;
And that was the time when our Little Boy Blue
    Kissed them and put them there.

'Now don't you go till I come,' he said,
    'And don't you make any noise!'
So, toddling off to his trundle bed,
    He dreamt of the pretty toys;
And, as he was dreaming, an angel song
    Awakened our Little Boy Blue —
Oh! the years are many, the years are long,
    But the little toy friends are true!
Ay, faithful to Little Boy Blue they stand,
    Each in the same old place,
Awaiting the touch of a little hand,
    The smile of a little face;
And they wonder, as waiting the long years through
    In the dust of that little chair,
What has become of our Little Boy Blue,
    Since he kissed them and put them there.

小小的玩具兵生锈发霉,
　　那支枪还握在手里。
小小的玩具狗新过一阵,
　　玩具兵也曾很漂亮;
那时我们蓝孩儿吻它们,
　　吻过后放在那地方。

"我回来前你们别走,"他讲,
　　"也别出一丁点声音!"
蹒跚的他走向带轮子小床,
　　走进好玩具的梦境;
他正在梦境里,天使唱的歌
　　把我们蓝孩儿唤醒——
过了这么久这么长的年月,
　　小玩具仍忠于友情!
是啊,他们听蓝孩儿吩咐,
　　各自都站在老地方——
等一只小手把它们摩抚,
　　等一张微笑小面庞;
等在积尘椅子里这么久,
　　它们的心里起疑惑:
蓝孩儿吻过它们放下后,
　　这些年来是怎么了?

EDWIN MARKHAM

Outwitted

He drew a circle that shut me out —
　　Heretic, rebel, a thing to flout.
But Love and I had the wit to win:
　　We drew a circle that took him in!

KATHARINE LEE BATES

America the Beautiful[1]

O beautiful, for spacious skies,
　　For amber waves of grain,
For purple mountain majesties
　　Above the fruited plain!
America! America!
　　God shed His grace on thee,
And crown thy good with brotherhood,
　　From sea to shining sea!

1　本诗写于19世纪90年代（后有修改），曾引起轰动，谱成六十多种曲子，特别流行的两种传唱至今。现在很多美国人主张以此为国歌。

马卡姆 (1852—1940)

棋高一着

他画了个圈,划我在圈外——
　　说异端、叛逆,该受到蔑视。
我和爱却用计把他打败:
　　我们画个圆,圈他在圆里。

凯瑟琳·李·贝茨 (1859—1929)

美丽的亚美利加

哦,美丽!这辽阔天空,
　　这琥珀色的麦浪,
这青紫色的山脉高耸
　　在果园般平原上!
亚美利加!亚美利加!
　　上帝赐恩惠于你:
闪烁两海间的兄弟情
　　是他最好的赐予!

O beautiful, for pilgrim feet[1]

　　Whose stern, impassioned stress

A thoroughfare for freedom beat

　　Across the wilderness!

America! America!

　　God mend thine every flaw;

Confirm thy soul in self control,

　　Thy liberty in law!

O beautiful, for heroes proved

　　In liberating strife,

Who more than self their country loved

　　And mercy more than life!

America! America!

　　May God thy gold refine,

Till all success be nobleness,

　　And every gain divine!

O beautiful, for patriot dream

　　That sees beyond the years,

Thine alabaster cities gleam

1　这里的 pilgrim 指美国早期移民，特别是清教徒前辈移民。

哦，美丽！老移民的脚
　　以坚定热切步伐，
为自由踏出一条大道，
　　把莽莽荒原横跨！
亚美利加！亚美利加！
　　你的缺陷主补救，
以自制使你的心坚定，
　　以法律巩固自由！

哦，美丽！解放斗争里
　　久经考验的英雄：
他们爱国家甚于自己，
　　爱仁慈甚于生命！
亚美利加！亚美利加！
　　愿主精炼你黄金，
炼到一切成就都高贵，
　　每种收获都神圣！

哦，美丽！爱国者怀着梦，
　　梦到今后多少年，
你那些洁白发亮城镇

Undimmed by human tears!

America! America!

　　God shed His grace on thee,

And crown thy good with brotherhood,

　　From sea to shining sea!

HARRIET MONROE

Love Song

I love my life, but not too well

　　To give it to thee like a flower,

So it may pleasure thee to dwell

　　Deep in its perfume but an hour.

I love my life, but not too well.

I love my life, but not too well

　　To sing it note by note away,

So to thy soul the song may tell

　　The beauty of the desolate day.

I love my life, but not too well.

I love my life, but not too well

不因眼泪而阴暗!
亚美利加! 亚美利加!
上帝赐恩惠于你,
闪烁两海间的兄弟情
是他最好的赐予!

哈丽叶特·门罗 (1860—1936)

恋歌

我爱生命,但不会舍不得
　　把它当成一朵花献给你,
让你在它的芳香中快乐,
　　哪怕只让你沉醉一小时。
我爱生命,但不会舍不得。

我爱生命,但不会舍不得
　　一个个音符来把它唱掉,
要把孤凄时日里的美色
　　唱得让你的灵魂能知道。
我爱生命,但不会舍不得。

我爱生命,但不会舍不得

To cast it like a cloak on thine,

Against the storms that sound and swell

  Between thy lonely heart and mine.

I love my life, but not too well.

FRANK DEMPSTER SHERMAN

A Quatrain

Hark at the lips of this pink whorl of shell

  And you shall hear the ocean's surge and roar:

So in the quatrain's measure, written well,

  A thousand lines shall all be sung in four!

EDGAR LEE MASTERS

'When under the Icy Eaves'

When under the icy eaves

  The swallow heralds the sun,

And the dove for its lost mate grieves,

  And the young lambs play and run;

When the sea is a plain of grass,

把它当斗篷裹在你身上，
帮你我寂寞的心儿阻遏
　　那呼啸其间的雨暴风狂。
我爱生命，但不会舍不得。

舍尔曼 (1860—1916)

一首四行诗

把耳朵凑近这粉红螺壳的嘴，
　　你就听见海洋的呼啸和汹涌；
同样，写得好的短短四行内，
　　也能够唱出一千行诗的内容。

马斯特斯 (1869—1950)

"当结冰的檐下燕子来"

当结冰的檐下燕子来，
　　把太阳的消息早宣告；
当鸽子为丧偶而悲哀，
　　当小羔羊玩耍又奔跑；
当海面像一大片草原，

And the blustering winds are still,

And the strength of the thin snows pass

    In the mists o'er the tawny hill —

The spirit of life awakes

In the fresh flags by the lakes.

EDWIN ARLINGTON ROBINSON

The Dark Hills

Dark hills at evening in the west,

    Where sunset hovers like a sound

Of golden horns that sang to rest

    Old bones of warriors under ground,

Far now from all the bannered ways

    Where flash the legions of the sun,

You fade—as if the last of days

    Were fading and all wars were done.

当怒吼的狂风已停止,
当残雪在赭色的山间
　在雾气下无力地消失——
瞧湖畔茁壮的新菖蒲,
知万物的生机已复苏。

罗宾森 (1869—1935)

幽暗的山丘

傍晚时西面幽暗的山丘!
　落日在你那里盘桓低回,
像黄金号角的齐声吹奏
　叫地下的武士骸骨安睡;
你现在离旌旗之路已远——
　那路上闪烁着阳光军团——
你在隐没,像最后的白天
　在隐没,而仗已全部打完。

JAMES WELDON JOHNSON

My City

When I come down to sleep death's endless night,
    The threshold of the unknown dark to cross,
    What to me then will be the keenest loss,
When this bright world blurs on my fading sight?
Will it be that no more I shall see the trees
    Or smell the flowers or hear the singing birds
    Or watch the flashing streams or patient herds?
No, I am sure it will be none of these.

But, ah! Manhattan's sights and sounds, her smells,
    Her crowds, her throbbing force, the thrill that comes
From being of her a part, her subtle spells,
    Her shining towers, her avenues, her slums—
        O God! The stark, unutterable pity,
        To be dead, and never again behold my city!

J. W. 约翰逊 (1871—1938)

我的城市

当我在死亡的无尽长夜睡下,
　　将越过门槛进入那未知黑暗——
　　那时光明世界已迷糊在眼前,
请想想,什么最让我割舍不下?
是不是从此再也见不到树木,
　　闻不到花香,听不见鸟雀歌唱,
　　看不到闪亮溪流和温驯牛羊?
对于这些,我可以肯定地说"不"。

而是曼哈顿的景观、声响、气息,
　　是她的人流、魅力和搏动力量,
是作为她一部分的那种奋激,
　　是她的辉煌高楼、大街和陋巷——
　　　　上帝呀,最难以接受的遗憾是:
　　　　死去后,永远见不到我这城市!

PAUL LAURENCE DUNBAR

Harriet Beecher Stowe[1]

She told the story, and the whole world wept
    At wrongs and cruelties it had not known
    But for this fearless woman's voice alone.
    She spoke to consciences that long had slept:
Her message, Freedom's clear reveille, swept
    From heedless hovel to complacent throne.
    Command and prophecy were in the tone
    And from its sheath the sword of justice leapt.
Around two peoples swelled a fiery wave,
    But both came forth transfigured from the flame.
Blest be the hand that dared be strong to save,
    And blest be she who in our weakness came —
Prophet and priestess! At one stroke she gave
    A race to freedom and herself to fame.

---

[1] Harriet Beecher Stowe (1811—1896) 常称斯陀夫人，1852 年发表小说《汤姆大伯的小屋》，揭露南方蓄奴制的罪恶和黑人奴隶的痛苦，引起强烈反响，第一年就印一百多版，售出三十多万册，对触发南北战争有一定影响。据说林肯总统称她为"写了一本书，酿成一场大战的小妇人"。

邓巴 (1872—1906)

哈丽叶特·比彻·斯陀

她讲的故事叫整个世界哭泣,
　　只有这无畏妇女的孤独声音
　　揭露不为人知的冤屈和残忍。
　　她向沉睡着的良知发出呼吁;
她响亮的晓角把自由的信息
　　传遍木然的陋室、自得的宫廷。
　　这晓角声中有着预言和命令,
　　叫人们抽剑出鞘去争取正义。
一片火海中曾卷入两个种族——
　　从火中出来时都已变了模样。
愿敢于拯救的强手永受祝福,
　　愿帮助我们弱者的常驻荣光——
这先知、祭司猛地把一个种族
　　送向自由,使自己也声名远扬。

ROBERT FROST

The Road Not Taken

Two roads diverged in a yellow wood,
And sorry I could not travel both
And be one traveler, long I stood
And looked down one as far as I could
To where it bent in the undergrowth;

Then took the other, as just as fair,
And having perhaps the better claim
Because it was grassy and wanted wear;
Though as for that, the passing there
Had worn them really about the same,

And both that morning equally lay
In leaves no step had trodden black.
Oh, I kept the first for another day!
Yet knowing how way leads on to way
I doubted if I should ever come back.

I shall be telling this with a sigh
Somewhere ages and ages hence:

弗罗斯特 (1874—1963)

没去走的路

两条路岔开在黄叶林子里,
可惜我一个人不能走两条;
我久久站立在那里,尽力地
沿其中的一条向前面望去,
只见它拐进矮树丛消失掉。

我选的另一条同样也很好,
很可能还有更大的吸引力,
因为招人去踩踏的草不少;
尽管在实际上,来往者的脚
给它们留下差不多的痕迹。

那一天早上,两条路在那里,
盖着路的落叶都没给踩脏。
头一条就留待以后的日子!
可是我知道路条条接下去——
今后还怎么能回到这地方?

在某个所在,过很久很久后,
我将会叹着气讲述这事情:

Two roads diverged in a wood, and I,

I took the one less traveled by,

And that has made all the difference.[1]

ADELAIDE CRAPSEY

On Seeing Weather-Beaten Trees

Is it as plainly in our living shown,

By slant and twist, which way the wind hath blown?

WALLACE STEVENS

Anecdote of the Jar

I placed a jar in Tennessee,[2]

And round it was, upon a hill.

It made the slovenly wilderness

---

1 作者在英国期间与诗人 Edward Thomas 友善,曾多次一起远足,1915年回国后,将本诗预发本寄给后者,作为对犹豫不决的打趣,因为后者远足时有此表现。让作者懊恼的是,读者大多未视之为打趣诗,特别是,这甚至促使后者参军,投入第一次世界大战,并在两年后阵亡。
2 田纳西州在美国中南部,东部多山,一半以上面积为森林覆盖。这里可能象征大自然。

在林中岔成两条路的路口，

我呀，我选了条人迹少的走，

而所有的差别由此就造成。

阿德莱德·克莱普西 (1878—1914)

见饱经风雨的树有感

凭着偏向与扭曲，我们生活中

不也清楚显现：刮过了什么风？

斯蒂文斯 (1879—1955)

坛子轶事

我在田纳西放了个坛子，

它圆圆的，放在小山上。

这就让芜杂散乱的荒野

Surround that hill.

The wilderness rose up to it,
And sprawled around, no longer wild,
The jar was round upon the ground
And tall and of a port in air.

It took dominion everywhere,
The jar was gray and bare.
It did not give of bird or bush,
Like nothing else in Tennessee.

GEORGIA DOUGLAS JOHNSON

'I Want to Die While You Love Me'

I want to die while you love me,
　　While yet you hold me fair,
While laughter lies upon my lips
　　And lights are in my hair.

I want to die while you love me
　　And bear to that still bed

围起那小山。

那荒野向着它挺立起来
并四处蔓延,不再蛮荒,
圆圆的坛子放在那地上,
高高的,显得庄重神气。

所有的地方都归它统制——
这灰色坛子没彩饰。
它并不产生鸟雀和树丛,
不像田纳西的其他事物。

乔治娅·道格拉斯·约翰逊 (1880—1966)

"我要在你爱我的时候死"

我要在你爱我的时候死,
　　趁你还认为我漂亮,
趁我嘴唇上还带着笑声,
　　发丝里还透着亮光。

我要在你爱我的时候死,
　　把你炽热未泯的吻

Your kisses turbulent, unspent
　　To warm me when I'm dead.

I want to die while you love me;
　　Oh, who would care to live
Till love has nothing more to ask
　　And nothing more to give?

I want to die while you love me,
　　And never, never see
The glory of this perfect day
　　Grow dim, or cease to be!

JOHN GNEISENAU NEIHARDT

'Let Me Live Out My Years in Heat of Blood'

Let me live out my years in heat of blood!

Let me lie drunken with the dreamer's wine!

Let me not see the soul-house built of mud

Go toppling to the dust — a vacant shrine.[1]

1　这节诗曾被杰克·伦敦用作其名著《马丁·伊登》的题诗。这里第一行译文来自吴劳先生的译本。

带到我静静安眠的地方，
　　把已死去的我温存。

我要在你爱我的时候死；
　　谁希罕活得那么久？——
活到爱再没什么能给予，
　　也再没什么能要求。

我要在你爱我的时候死；
　　这日子光辉又美满，
我绝对不忍看着它消失，
　　看着它渐渐变暗淡！

奈哈特 (1881—1973)

"让我在热血沸腾中度此一生"

让我在热血沸腾中度此一生！
让我酣饮了美梦之酒便醉卧！
别让我眼见容纳灵魂的泥身
跌落尘土时只是空虚的躯壳。

Let me go quickly, like a candle light

Snuffed out just at the heyday of its glow.

Give me high noon — and let it then be night!

Thus would I go.

And grant that when I face the grisly Thing,

My song may trumpet down the grey Perhaps.

O let me be a tune-swept fiddle string

That feels the Master Melody — and snaps!

EDGAR A. GUEST

It Can't Be Done

Somebody said that it couldn't be done,

    But he, with a chuckle, replied

That 'maybe it couldn't', but he would be one

    Who wouldn't say so till he tried.

So he buckled right in with a trace of a grin[1]

    On his face, if he worried he hid it.

He started to sing as he tackled the thing

---

1 本诗各节的第 5 与第 7 行分别用同一个词结尾,而且都用行中韵。

让我像一支蜡烛突然间熄灭,
让它光华四射时被掐掉烛芯。
让我像正午,让它接着是黑夜!
这样去,才称心。

面对死神时,让我的歌像号角
能响彻那灰蒙蒙的未知世界。
让我是提琴的琴弦倾泻曲调——
体验那至高旋律时啪地断却!

格斯特 (1881—1959)

这不可能完成

有人说过,这事情干不成。
　　但他格格一笑说:
是可能干不成,不过他不肯
　　这么说,除非他试过。
他心到手也到,咧嘴笑了笑,
　　要担心,也藏在心中。
他一边干起来,一边唱起来,

That couldn't be done — and he did it.

Somebody scoffed: 'Oh, you'll never do that;
    At least no one ever has done it.'
But he took off his coat and he took off his hat,
    And the first thing we knew he'd begun it.
With the lift of his chin, and a bit of a grin,
    Without any doubting or quiddit.
He started to sing as he tackled the thing
    That couldn't be done, and he did it.

There are thousands to tell you it cannot be done;
    There are thousands to prophesy failure;
There are thousands to point out to you, one by one,
    The dangers that wait to assail you.
But just buckle in with a bit of a grin,
    Just take off your coat and go to it;
Just start to sing as you tackle the thing
    That 'cannot be done', and you'll do it.

干不成的事情他完成。

有人冷言道,"你永远干不成;
　　至少还没人能成功。"
他把帽一脱,把外套一扔,
　　只见他已经在行动。
他的头昂得高,咧嘴笑了笑,
　　没一点迟疑和争论。
他一边干起来,一边唱起来;
　　干不成的事情他完成。

千百人会说,这不可能完成;
　　千百人会预言你失败;
千百人会一个个向你指明,
　　有多少艰险在等待。
但心到手也到,咧嘴笑一笑,
　　把外套脱了干事情;
　一边唱起来,一边干起来;
　　"干不成的事"你完成。

WILLIAM CARLOS WILLIAMS

The Red Wheelbarrow

so much depends

upon

a red wheel

barrow

glazed with rain

water

beside the white

chickens[1]

---

[1] 这首我国读者最熟悉的现代诗体现了格律上的探索，是"计词诗"（counted verse）最著名的例子，也即诗行长短以"词"计量，不以音步或音节计。如本诗中单行均为三个词，双行均为一个词（不问词的长短、也不问是虚词还是实词）。这同后面的"音节诗"一样，表明诗人们在自由诗之后摸索新格律的尝试。当然对这种格律诗的翻译也要摸索。

威廉斯 (1883—1963)

红颜色手推小车

多少事依靠

一辆

红颜色手推

小车——

雨水中闪着

亮光

边上是几只

白鸡

SARA TEASDALE

Let It Be Forgotten

Let it be forgotten, as a flower is forgotten,
  Forgotten as a fire that once was singing gold,
Let it be forgotten for ever and ever,
  Time is a kind friend, he will make us old.

If anyone asks, say it was forgotten
  Long and long ago,
As a flower, as a fire, as a hushed footfall
  In a long-forgotten snow.

ELINOR WYLIE

Let No Charitable Hope

Now let no charitable hope

Confuse my mind with images

Of eagle and of antelope:

I am in nature none of these.

I was, being human, born alone;

萨拉·蒂斯代尔 (1884—1933)

让它被遗忘

让它被遗忘,像遗忘一朵花儿,
　　像遗忘一度欢唱的金色火苗;
让它被遗忘,被永远永远遗忘——
　　时间是个好朋友,它催我们老。

若有人问起,就说它已被遗忘,
　　说很久前已被忘记——
就像一朵花,一团火,一个脚步声
　　在早被遗忘的雪里。

埃莉诺·怀利 (1885—1928)

别让仁慈的希望

如今,别让仁慈的希望
凭借羚羊和鹰的形象
把我的心思搅浑弄乱:
我的本性同这些无缘。

我因为是人,天生孤单;

I am, being woman, hard beset;

I live by squeezing from a stone

The little nourishment I get.

In masks outrageous and austere

The years go by in single file;

But none has merited my fear,

And none has quite escaped my smile.[1]

EZRA POUND

A Virginal

No, no! Go from me. I have left her lately.

    I will not spoil my sheath with lesser brightness,

    For my surrounding air hath a new lightness;

Slight are her arms, yet they have bound me straitly

And left me cloaked as with a gauze of aether;

    As with sweet leaves; as with subtle clearness.

    Oh, I have picked up magic in her nearness

To sheathe me half in half the things that sheathe her.

1　本诗韵式为 abab，但译文韵式为 aabb，不甚理想。为表明韵式有异，译文采用"齐头"排列。

我又是女人,多灾多难;
岩石里榨出一点水浆
是我赖以生存的营养。

蒙着强暴严酷的面具,
一列岁月在眼前过去,
但,没什么值得我惊慌
或逃过我的含笑目光。

庞德 (1885—1972)

一架少女琴

不不!走开吧。她才刚刚离开我。
  我不愿笼罩我的光辉受损害,
  因为包容我的空气新添光彩;
她双臂纤细,却曾紧紧搂住我,
像是让我穿上了灵气般轻罗,
  像穿上芬芳树叶和隐约清晰。
  我呀从她的亲近中获得魔力,
使一半裹着她的一半裹着我。

No, no! Go from me. I have still the flavour,

　　Soft as spring wind that's come from birchen bowers.

　　　　Green come the shoots, aye April in the branches,

　　　　As winter's wound with her sleight hand she staunches,

Hath of the trees a likeness of the savour:

　　As white their bark, so white this lady's hours.

ALFRED JOYCE KILMER

Tree

I think that I shall never see

A poem lovely as a tree.

A tree whose hungry mouth is prest

Against the earth's sweet flowing breast;

A tree that looks at god all day

And lifts her leafy arms to pray;

A tree that may in summer wear

A nest of robins in her hair;

不不！走开吧。我仍带着那香味——
　像白桦丛中吹来的柔和春风。
　　嫩芽爆青，是啊，树枝间的四月
　　　像她巧手给冬天的创伤止血，
这少女有着白桦树那种风味：
　她的光阴正如那树皮的白净。

基尔默 (1886—1918)

树

我想，永远见不到一首诗
能有一棵树那样的韵致。

树的嘴饥渴地贴着大地，
把地下甘美的乳汁吮吸；

树整天整天凝视着上苍，
祈祷中举着叶茸茸臂膀；

树的头发里可以有个巢，
夏日里巢中有窝知更鸟；

Upon whose bosom snow has lain,

Who intimately lives with rain.

Poems are made by fools like me,

But only God can make a tree.

MARIANNE MOORE

A Talisman

Under a splintered mast,

torn from the ship and cast

  near her hull,

a stumbling shepherd found,

embedded in the ground,

  a sea-gull

of lapis lazuli,

a scarab of the sea,[1]

  with wings spread —

---

1   scarab 意为古埃及人用宝石或彩陶等材料做的甲虫形护符或装饰品。这里的天青石海鸥之于航海人,正如甲虫形护符之于(陆上的)古埃及人。

雪花曾躺在树的胸怀间,
树同雨的相处也很亲善。

作诗的是我这样的蠢货,
而只有上苍能把树制作。

玛丽安娜·穆尔 (1887—1972)

一个护符

离破船不远的地方,
那桅杆断落在地上,
　　已残碎支离,

牧羊人在那里一绊,
发现断桅下的沙间
　　埋着件东西:

那是个天青石海鸥;
这航海人用的护符
　　展开着翅膀,

curling its coral feet,

parting its beak to greet

 men long dead.[1]

JOHN CROWE RANSOM

Piazza Piece

—I am a gentleman in a dustcoat trying[2]

 To make you hear. Your ears are soft and small

 And listen to an old man not at all,

They want the young men's whispering and sighing.

But see the roses on your trellis dying

 And hear the spectral singing of the moon;

 For I must have my lovely lady soon,

I am a gentleman in a dustcoat trying.

—I am a lady young in beauty waiting

 Until my truelove comes, and then we kiss.

 But what grey man among the vines is this

---

1 本诗韵式为 aab ccb dde ffe。这样的格律由古老的尾韵诗节（tail rhyme stanza）化出——再追溯上去，则来自法国原型 rime couée。
2 这首诗是"死神和少女"的现代版。

蜷缩着珊瑚色双脚,

张着嘴向人们问好——

  人早已死亡。

兰瑟姆 (1888—1974)

廊下曲

  ——我是穿挡尘风衣的绅士,想请你
   听听我的话。你两只软软小耳朵
   根本就不会听一个老汉的劝说,
 却要年青人的轻言巧语和叹息。
 但看看棚架上的玫瑰奄奄待毙,
   听听月亮发出的幽魂般的歌唱;
   因为我得快一点得到可爱女郎,
 我是穿挡尘风衣的绅士,想请你……

  ——我是等候着的年轻貌美的女郎,
   要等到我情人来和我拥抱亲吻。
   但藤蔓间的这个老头是什么人?

Whose words are dry and faint as in a dream?

Back from my trellis, Sir, before I scream!

I am a lady young in beauty waiting.

CONRAD AIKEN

A Sonnet

Think, when a starry night of bitter frost
　　Is ended, and the small pale winter sun
Shines on the garden trellis, ice-embossed,
　　And the stiff frozen flowers-stalks, every one,
And turns their fine embroideries of ice
　　Into a loosening silver, skein by skein,
Warming cold sticks and stones, till, in a trice,
　　The garden sighs, and smiles, and breathes again:

And further think how the poor frozen snail
　　Creeps out with trembling horn to feel the heat,
And thaws the snowy mildew from his mail,
　　Stretching with all his length from his retreat:
Will he not praise, with his whole heart, the sun?
Then think at last I too am such an one.

他的话干涩而轻幽,如梦呓一般。

　　快离开我棚架,先生,免得我大喊!

我是等候着的年轻貌美的女郎。

艾肯 (1889—1973)

一首十四行诗

你想想,当霜重星朗的夜结束,
　　当一轮小小淡淡的冬日太阳
照着花园里结有冰花的棚柱,
　　照在每根冻得僵硬的花梗上,
把它们那些精细的冰霜锦绣
　　融化成一溜一溜银子般液体,
渐渐焐热冰冷的枝条和石头,
　　一转眼,花园微笑着重新呼吸:

你再想想冻僵了的可怜蜗牛
　　抖动着触角爬出来感受温暖,
让甲壳上的雪花斑化为乌有,
　　让蜗居里的身子能充分伸展:
他可会全心全意地赞美太阳?
然后想想我,我同他不也一样?

CLAUDE MCKAY

If We Must Die[1]

If we must die, let it not be like hogs

    Hunted and penned in an inglorious spot,

While round us bark the mad and hungry dogs

    Making their mock at our accursed lot;

If we must die, O let us nobly die,

    So that our precious blood may not be shed

In vain; then even the monsters we defy

    Shall be constrained to honour us though dead.

O kinsmen! We must meet the common foe!

    Though far outnumbered let us show us brave,

And for their thousand blows, deal one death blow!

    What though before us lies the open grave?

Like men we'll face the murderous, cowardly pack,

Pressed to the wall, dying, but fighting back!

---

1 美国在1919年发生过种族骚乱的浪潮，十多个城市里白人袭击了黑人社区。本诗因此而写。第二次世界大战中，英军被迫从法国的敦刻尔克大撤退，英国首相丘吉尔向议会报告时引用了该诗，使之有了新的意义。

麦凯 (1890—1948)

如果我们必须死

如果我们必须死,别死得像猪——
　　被追逐驱赶,关进可耻的猪笼,
而四周那些疯狂吠叫的饿狗
　　把我们可憎可悲的命运嘲弄;
如果我们必须死,要死得高贵,
　　让我们宝贵的热血不是白淌,
即便死,也让我们抗击的恶鬼
　　对我们只能报以敬重的目光。
同胞们!我们得迎战共同死敌!
　　众寡悬殊正显出我们的英勇,
以致命一击还他们万千打击!
　　哪怕面前就是个露天的坟坑!
男子汉虽退到墙角,奄奄一息,
对凶残怯懦的群敌,仍在反击!

EDNA ST. VINCENT MILLAY

The Spring and the Fall

In the spring of the year, in the spring of the year,
I walked the road beside my dear.
The trees were black where the bark was wet.
I see them yet, in the spring of the year.
He broke me a bough of the blossoming peach
That was out of the way and hard to reach.

In the fall of the year, in the fall of the year,
I walked the road beside my dear.
The rooks went up with a raucous trill.
I hear them still, in the fall of the year.
He laughed at all I dared to praise
And broke my heart, in little ways.

Year be spring or year be falling,
The bark will drip and the birds be calling.
There's much that's fine to see and hear
In the spring of a year, in the fall of a year.
'Tis not love's going hurt my days,
But that it went in little ways.

爱德哪·圣文森特·米莱 (1892—1950)

春与秋

在那年春天,在那年春天,
我走在路上,爱人在身边。
那树皮湿湿的黢黑树木。
我依然还看见那年春天。
在路旁,他在很难够到处,
摘给我盛开的桃花一株。

在那年秋天,在那年秋天,
我走在路上,爱人在身边。
嘎嘎叫声中飞起白嘴鸦。
我仍然能听见那年秋天。
我敢于赞美的一切事情
他取笑,这让我有点伤心。

无论春勃兴,无论秋凋零,
树皮会滴水,鸟雀会啼鸣。
在一年之春,在一年之秋,
美景和佳音处处都会有。
日子难过倒不是没了爱,
却是爱逐渐逐渐地离开。

ROBERT PETER TRISTRAM COFFIN

The Secret Heart

Across the years he could recall
His father one way best of all.

In the stillest hour of night
The boy awakened to a light.

Half in dreams he saw his sire
With his great hands full of fire.

The man had struck a match to see
If his son slept peacefully.

He held his palms each side the spark,
His love had kindled in the dark.

His two hands were curved apart
In the semblance of a heart.

He wore, it seemed to his small son,
A bare heart on his hidden one.

科芬 (1892—1955)

秘藏的心

隔了这些年要回忆爸爸,
他有着一个最好的方法。

在那黑夜里最寂静时刻,
一点儿亮光使孩子醒了。

他父亲似乎在梦中浮现——
一双大手中有火光一团。

是他擦了根火柴凑着亮,
看一看他儿子睡得可香。

他两个手掌拢着那团火,
他的爱在那黑暗中烧灼;

分开着的两个弯曲手掌,
那也正是一颗心的模样。

在他那年幼的儿子看来,
他的心分成了一里一外。

A heart that gave out such a glow

No son awake could bear to know.

It showed a look upon a face

Too tender for the day to trace.

One instant, it lit all about,

And then the secret heart went out.

But it shone long enough for one

To know that hands held up the sun.

ARCHIBALD MACLEISH

Immortal Autumn

I speak this poem now with grave and level voice

In praise of autumn of the far-horn-winding fall

I praise the flower-barren fields the clouds the tall

Unanswering branches where the winds make sullen noise

I praise the fall it is the human season now

No more the foreign sun does meddle at our earth

一颗心发出如此的光焰,
醒着的儿子见了难心安。

它照出脸上的那种神情
过于纤柔,白天反看不清。

霎时间它照亮周围一切,
随即这秘藏的心已熄灭。

但它照亮的时间已够长,
儿子已看见双手捧太阳。

麦克利什 (1892—1982)

不朽的秋

我现在用庄严平缓的声音宣读这诗
以赞美秋天这远处响着猎号的秋天
我赞美无花的田野云天和对林木间
沉闷的呼呼风声不予回答的高树枝

我赞美这落叶季节它充满人性如今
异域的太阳不再来干预我们的大地

Enforce the green and thaw the frozen soil to birth

Nor winter yet weigh all with silence the pine bough

But now in autumn with the black and outcast crows

Share we the spacious world the whispering year is gone

There is more room to live now the once secret dawn

Comes late by daylight and the dark unguarded goes

Between the mutinous brave burning of the leaves

And winter's covering of our hearts with his deep snow

We are alone there are no evening birds we know

The naked moon the tame stars circle at our eaves

It is the human season on this sterile air

Do words outcarry breath the sound goes on and on

I hear a dead man's cry from autumn long since gone

I cry to you beyond this bitter air.[1]

1　本诗仅此一个句号,中间没有标点。

硬逼出青翠还融开冻土焕发出生机
而冬天还没有给一切松枝压上寂静

如今秋天里我们与被撇下的黑乌鸦
分享这寥廓世界窘窄的时日已过去
现在生活的天地大一度隐秘的晨曦
随白天迟来而黑暗不受注意地退下

在反叛的树叶绚烂得如同火烧一样
和冬日厚雪盖上我们心头这两者间
我们很寂寞没我们认识的晚鸟出现
而裸露的月温顺的星周转在屋檐旁

这是人性的季节在这贫瘠的空气里
言词传得比气息远这声音越传越远
在久逝的秋中我听见一位死者在喊
我越过这凛冽的空气呼唤你。

E. E. CUMMINGS[1]

'Me Up at Does'

Me up at does

out of the floor

quietly Stare

a poisoned mouse

still who alive

is asking What

have i done that

You wouldn't have[2]

ROSEMARY and STEPHEN BENÉT

Western Wagons

They went with axe and rifle, when the trail was still to blaze

They went with wife and children, in the prairie-schooner days

---

[1] 这位诗人以别出心裁著名,连自己姓名也用小写字母。当然,本诗中的大小写值得注意。

[2] 本诗每行四音节,韵式为 a bb a c dd c,但"押韵"的是行末辅音。诗的头五行中,正常的词序被打乱,表示说话人因心情慌乱而语无伦次。

肯明斯 (1894—1962)

"抬头盯视我"

抬头盯视我

从地板缝隙

中毒的耗子

居然还活着

沉静的眼神

是在问我话

我干了点啥

惹您不高兴

勃耐夫妇 (1898—1943,1898—1962)

西行的大篷车

路还在开拓,他们已带着枪和斧头出发,

他们走在那大篷车时代,带上了一个家,

With banjo and with frying pan—Susanna, don't you cry![1]
For I'm off to California to get rich out there or die!

We've broken land and cleared it, but we're tired of where we are.
They say that wild Nebraska is a better place by far.
There's gold in far Wyoming, there's black earth in Ioway,[2]
So pack up the kids and blankets, for we're moving out today.

The cowards never started and the weak died on the road,
And all across the continent the endless campfires glowed.
We'd taken land and settled—but a traveler passed by—
And we're going West tomorrow—Lordy, never ask us why!

We're going West tomorrow, where the promises can't fail.
O'er the hills in legions, boys, and crowd the dusty trail!
We shall starve and freeze and suffer. We shall die, and tame the lands.
But we're going West tomorrow, with our fortune in our hands.

---

1 "Oh, Susanna" 是深受人民喜爱的美国作曲家 Stephen Foster (1826—1864) 的名曲，其中有脍炙人口的歌词：Oh! Susanna, oh! don't you cry for me, for I come from Alabama with my banjo on my knee。这首歌的大普及与加利福尼亚的淘金热有关。
2 Nebraska, Wyoming, Ioway (即 Iowa) 都是美国西部的州名。

还带班卓琴和平底锅——苏珊娜,你不要哭泣!
我要到加利福尼亚去发家,或死在那里!

我们开垦了土地,但已经厌倦了这地方。
人家说内布拉斯加好得多,尽管很荒凉。
遥远的怀俄明出金子,艾奥瓦到处是黑土,
快打点好孩子和铺盖,我们今天就上路。

胆小鬼从来不远行,病弱的就死在路上,
这大陆东到西,都有无尽的篝火放着光。
我们拿了地就待下——但只要是有人经过——
明天就往西去——老天哪,千万别问为什么!

第二天就往西去,去让人不会失望的地方。
弟兄们,去翻山越岭,拥挤在灰蒙蒙小道上!
我们将挨饿受冻或死去,将开垦出耕地。
但明天就要再往西,命运在自己的手里。

MALCOLM COWLEY

The Farm Died

I watched the agony of a mountain farm,

a gangrenous decay:

the farm died with the pines that sheltered it;

the farm died when the woodshed rotted away.

It died to the beat of a loose board on the barn

That flapped in the wind all night;

Nobody came to drive a nail in it.

The farm died in a broken window-light,

a broken pane upstairs in the guest bedroom,

through which the autumn rain

beat down all night upon the Turkey carpet;

nobody thought to putty in a pane.

Nobody nailed another slat on the corncrib;

nobody mowed the hay;

nobody came to mend the rusty fences.

The farm died when the two boys went away,

考利 (1898—1989)

死去的农庄

我眼看山间农庄死去时的痛苦,
那是坏疽般的衰败:
那农舍同护卫它的松林一起死;
死去的时候柴火棚也朽烂塌坏。

谷仓松脱的板整夜在风中拍打——
农庄按这节拍死亡;
但没有人来用钉子把那板钉牢。
农舍就死在一方破碎玻璃窗上——

楼上的客房里有块玻璃碎掉了,
秋雨就从那窗洞里
整夜打进来,打在土耳其地毯上;
却没人想到用油灰粘上块玻璃。

没有人给玉米穗库房再钉板条;
没有人再收割牧草;
也没人来修理破破烂烂的栅栏。
这农庄就死于两个小伙子走掉,

or maybe lived till the old man was buried,

but after it was dead I loved it more,

thought poison sumac grew in the empty pastures,

though ridgepoles fell, and though November winds

came all night whistling through an open door.

ERNEST HEMINGWAY

The Age Demanded

The age demanded that we sing

And cut away our tongue.

The age demanded that we flow

And hammered in the bung.

The age demanded that we dance

And jammed us into iron pants.

And in the end the age was handed

The sort of shit that it demanded.

也可说活到那老汉入土的时候，
但是这死后的农庄我倒更加爱，
尽管空荡荡牧场上长起毒漆树，
尽管大梁已塌下而十一月的风
整夜从敞开的门口呼哨着吹来。

海明威 (1899—1961)

这时代曾要求

这时代曾要求我们唱歌
却割掉了我们舌头。

这时代曾要求我们畅饮
却敲紧酒桶上塞头。

这时代曾要求我们起舞，
却硬把我们塞进铁长裤。

最后这时代得到的东西
是它要求的那种臭垃圾。

LANGSTON HUGHES

Dreams

Hold fast to dreams

For if dreams die

Life is a broken winged bird

That cannot fly.

Hold fast to dreams

For when dreams go

Life is a barren field

Frozen with snow.

OGDEN NASH

Love under the Republicans

(or Democrats)

Come live with me and be my love

And we will all the pleasures prove[1]

Of a marriage conducted with economy

1　这两行来自英国诗人马洛 The Passionate Shepherd to His Love 一诗（见前）开头，是现代诗人对该诗的反应。

休斯 (1902—1967)

梦

紧紧抱住梦;
要是梦死亡,
生活便是断翅鸟
再不能飞翔。

紧紧抱住梦;
要是梦离开,
生活就是不毛地
被冰雪覆盖。

纳什 (1902—1971)

共和党下的爱情

(或民主党下的)

来与我同住,做我的爱人,
我们要精打细算结个婚,
在这耶稣金元二十世纪

In the Twentieth Century Anno Donomy.[1]

We'll live in a dear little walk-up flat
With practically room to swing a cat
And a potted cactus to give it hauteur
And a bathtub equipped with dark brown water.

We'll eat, without undue discouragement,
Foods low in cost but high in nouragement[2]
And quaff with pleasure, while chatting wittily,
The peculiar wine of Little Italy.[3]

We'll remind each other it's smart to be thrifty
And buy our clothes for something-fifty.
We'll stand in line on holidays
For seats at unpopular matinees.

1　耶稣纪元（或公元）在英语中应为 Anno Domini，这里作者故意误拼，就与上一行押了三重韵，而押这种韵往往有讽刺或滑稽的效果。
2　nouragement 应是 nourishment 的故意误拼，而与上一行的 discouragement 押韵，因此译文中把"营养"写成"阴阳"。
3　Little Italy，大城市中意大利移民或意大利裔居民较集中的区域，纽约就有这样的"小意大利"。

体验到婚姻的全部甜蜜。

我们要住在温馨小阁楼,
那大小遛遛猫正好还够,
放盆仙人掌能显出气派,
澡盆能放出深棕色水来。

我们吃低价高阴阳食品,
没理由感到泄气或扫兴;
我们喝着酒,俏皮地交谈,
把私酿的怪酒朝肚里灌。

我们常互勉:节俭是美德,
买衣服至少要打个对折。
我们为节假日场票排队——
这场次冷门,能有个座位。

For every Sunday we'll have a lark

And take a walk in Central Park.

And one of these days not too remote

I'll probably up and cut your throat.

KENNETH REXROTH

Song for a Dancer

I dream my love goes riding out

Upon a coal black mare.

A cloud of dark all about

Her — her floating hair.

She wears a short green velvet coat.

Her blouse is of red silk,

Open to her swan like throat,

Her breasts white as milk.

Her skirt is of green velvet, too,

And shows her silken thigh,

Purple leather for her shoe,

Dark as her blue eye.

每个星期天我们要游玩,
去中央公园里走走转转。
可能在并不远的某一天,
我心头火起,割断你喉管。

瑞克斯罗思 (1905—1982)

为一位舞者而唱

我梦见情人骑着马出门,
骑着煤样黑的母马。
她周围大团的浓云
是她飘扬的长发。

她穿着一件绿丝绒短衫,
衬衣的料子是红绸,
敞开在天鹅般颈前,
露出乳白的胸口。

她还穿一条绿丝绒裙子,
露出的大腿像素锦;
脚上的皮鞋深紫色,
深得像她蓝眼睛。

From her saddle grows a rose.

She rides in scented shade.

Silver birds sing as she goes

This song that she made:

'My father was a nightingale,

My mother a mermaid.

Honeyed notes that never fail

Upon my lips they laid.'

WYSTAN HUGH AUDEN

Song of the Master and Boatswain

At Dirty Dick's and Sloppy Joe's

    We drank our liquor straight,

Some went upstairs with Margery,

    And some, alas, with Kate;[1]

And two by two like cat and mouse

---

[1] 莎士比亚《暴风雨》中有一首短歌,头四行如下:
The master, the swabber, the boatswain and I,
The gunner and his mate,
Loved Mall, Meg, and Marian and Margery,
But none of us cared for Kate.

一株玫瑰长在她马鞍上。
她就骑行在香荫里。
她边骑，银色鸟边唱，
唱的是她作的曲：

"我的父亲是一只夜莺，
我母亲是条美人鱼。
蜜样的听不厌歌声
他们给我这闺女。"

奥登 (1907—1973)

船长和水手长之歌

在腌臜狄克、邋遢乔那里
　　我们曾不停喝烈酒，
有人就挽玛杰丽去楼上，
　　也有人同凯蒂上楼；
一双双像猫和老鼠一样，

The homeless played at keeping house.

There Wealthy Meg, the Sailor's friend,
 And Marion, cow-eyed,
Opened their arms to me but I
 Refused to step inside;
I was not looking for a cage
In which to mope in my old age.

The nightingales are sobbing in
 The orchards of our mothers,
And hearts that we broke long ago
 Have long been breaking others;
Tears are round, the sea is deep:
Roll them overboard and sleep.

THEODORE ROETHKE

My Papa's Waltz

The whiskey on your breath

Could make a small boy dizzy,

But I hung on like death:

无家者要把家的滋味尝。

外号水手之友的阔梅格
　和牛眼姑娘玛莉恩，
都曾张开了怀抱欢迎我，
　我可是拒绝了她们；
因为我不是在寻找牢笼，
不想在年老时呆在其中。

我们母亲的那些果园里，
　一只只夜莺啼声悲，
很久前被我们揉碎的心
　很早让别人也心碎；
泪珠儿滚圆，海又深又大：
让泪珠滚落海里就睡吧。

瑞特克 (1908—1963)

我爸爸的华尔兹

你的威士忌酒气
能熏得小男孩醉掉；
可我死命吊住你：

Such waltzing was not easy.

We romped until the pans
Slid from the kitchen shelf;
My mother's countenance
Could not unfrown itself.

The hand that held my wrist
Was battered on one knuckle;
At every step you missed
My right ear scraped a buckle.

You beat time on my head
With a palm caked hard by dirt,
Then waltzed me off to bed
Still clinging to your shirt.

ELIZABETH BISHOP

One Art

The art of losing isn't hard to master;
so many things seem filled with the intent

这种华尔兹很难跳。

我们这跳跳蹦蹦
让平底锅滑下厨架;
再看妈妈那表情——
纠结的眉头没变化。

你的指关节断过——
握我手腕的是那手;
你只要一步跳错,
我右耳就擦到纽扣。

在我头上打拍子——
你掌上污垢硬邦邦;
我虽拉着你衬衣,
你跳着舞送我上床。

伊丽莎白·毕晓普 (1911—1979)

一种艺术

丢失是一种艺术,掌握并不难;
看来,许多事物本准备被丢失,

to be lost that their loss is no disaster.

Lose something every day. Accept the fluster
of lost door keys, the hour badly spent.
The art of losing isn't hard to master.

Then practice losing farther, losing faster:
places, and names, and where it was you meant
to travel. None of these will bring disaster.[1]

I lost my mother's watch. And look! my last, or
next-to-last, of three loved houses went.
The art of losing isn't hard to master.

I lost two cities, lovely ones. And, vaster,
some realms I owned, two rivers, a continent.
I miss them, but it wasn't a disaster.

— Even losing you (the joking voice, a gesture
I love) I shan't have lied. It's evident

---

1 本诗这种诗体是来自法国的 villanelle（维拉内尔），这里的第 9、第 15、第 19 行中只重复第 3 行最末一词，而非整行重复，这是现代诗人对此传统诗体的继承和发展。

所以说，丢失它们绝不是灾难。

每天丢失点东西。接受那不安：
如糟蹋钟点或者丢失门钥匙。
丢失是一种艺术，掌握并不难。

然后，就会丢失得更快也更远：
地点、名称和你想去的旅游地。
所有这一切，都不会带来灾难。

我丢失了母亲的表。我很喜欢
那三栋房屋，瞧！却几乎全丧失。
丢失是一种艺术，掌握并不难。

我丢失两座城，很美。这还不算：
还有两条河、一个洲，我的领域。
我思念它们，不过这不是灾难。

你逗乐的嗓音、姿势我虽喜欢，
但我不会撒谎，即便是丢失你。

the art of losing's not too hard to master

though it may look like (*Write it!*) like disaster.

DUDLEY RANDALL

The Melting Pot

There is a magic melting pot

where any girl or man

can step in Czech or Greek or Scot,[1]

step out American.

Johann and *Jan* and *Juan*,

Giovanni and *Ivan*

step in and then step out again

all freshly christened *John*.

Sam, watching, said, 'Why, I was here

even before they came,'

and stepped in too, but was tossed out

---

[1] 本诗以规范的谣曲诗节写成,单行四音步八音节(双行三音步六音节),为符合这要求,这行诗中用了 Czech、Greek、Scot 这样三个单音节词。现在这行诗的译文虽然四顿,但字数大大"超额",如需符合译文中单行四顿十字(双行三顿八字)的要求,可译成"进去时说法语、德语、俄语"。

显然,丢失的艺术掌握不太难,
尽管可能看来像(写下!)像灾难。

兰德尔 (1914—2000)

大熔炉

这是一个奥妙的大熔炉,
不管是哪里来的人,
进去是捷克人、希腊人、苏格兰人,
出来时都是美国人。

不管是胡安、是扬、是若望,
或是乔凡尼和伊凡,
进去后出来就都改了名,
那新的教名是约翰。

山姆看到这一点,一边说
"他们都比我来得晚",
一边跨进去,但还没进去

before he passed the brim.

And every time Sam tried that pot

they threw him out again.

'Keep out. This is our private pot.

We don't want your black stain.

At last, thrown out a thousand times,

Sam said, 'I don't give a damn.

Shove your old pot. You can like it or not,

but I'll be just what I am.'

GWENDOLYN BROOKS

We Real Cool[1]

The Pool Player,

Seven at the Golden Shovel.[2]

We real cool. We

---

1 本诗形式特殊,除"我们"外,两行一韵(头韵也多)而用语俚俗,因为"说话人"是泡在弹子房里的校外小混混。cool 一词本来很难用一个汉字表达,但现在有了相应的"酷"(甚至还发展出"酷毙了"),可见,随着文化交流和语言发展,有些被认为不可译的东西未必一成不变。
2 "弹子房"现可称"桌球房",以前很普遍,其中灯光暗淡,往往还有酒吧。桌球可用来赌博,而赌博中,"七"是个吉利的数字。

他就被抛到了外面。

山姆一次又一次想进去,
但每次都被抛出来。
"这是专用炉,不要你黑料。
别进来把我们搞坏。"

山姆被这样抛出一千次,
最后说"我才不在乎。
任你喜不喜欢,我就这样。
去你的这个老熔炉"。

格温德琳·布鲁克斯 (1917—2000)

咱们真酷

打落袋的人,

七点钟在金铲弹子房

咱们真酷。咱们

Left school. We

Lurk late. We
Strike straight. We

Sing sin. We
Thin gin. We

Jazz June. We[1]
Die soon.

HOWARD NEMEROV

An Old Story

They gathered shouting crowds along the road

To praise His majesty satin and cloth of gold,

　　But 'Naked! Naked!' the children cried.

Now when the gaudy clothes ride down the street

No child is found sufficiently indiscreet

　　To whisper 'No majesty's inside.'

1　Jazz June 也可意为"使六月过得有劲"等。

不去读书。咱们

泡到老晚。咱们
快速出拳。咱们

歌唱犯罪。咱们
给酒掺水。咱们

同琼睡觉。咱们
很快死掉。

内梅罗夫 (1920—1991)

一个老故事

他们沿街把欢呼的人群聚集,
赞美国王陛下的锦缎金缕衣,
　　但孩子们叫道:"没穿衣裳!"

如今当奇装艳服在招摇过市,
　找不到一个足够轻率的孩子
　　会轻声咕哝:"里面不高档。"

RICHARD WILBUR

Candid

Life is happiness indeed

Mares to ride and books to read

Though of noble birth I'm not

I'm delighted with my lot

Though I've no distinctive features

And I've no official mother

I love all my fellow creatures

And the creatures love each other

LOUIS SIMPSON

To the Western World

A siren sang, and Europe turned away

From the high castle and the shepherd's crook.

Three caravels went sailing to Cathay[1]

On the strange ocean, and the captains shook

---

1 caravels 指 15 到 17 世纪西班牙和葡萄牙那种轻快多桅帆船。哥伦布 1492 年 8 月 3 日率三艘这种船从帕洛斯角（见第 8 行）出发。

威尔伯 (1921—2017)

率真

人生也的确是幸福

可以骑骑马看看书

虽说我出身不高贵

对这种命运却无悔

虽说我相貌不出众

又没有正式的母亲

我却爱所有的生灵

而生灵也相爱相亲

辛普森 (1923—2012)

致西方世界

汽笛一唱,欧洲从羊倌的曲柄杖

和巍峨的城堡扭转了身子走开。

三艘多桅小帆船在陌生大洋上

要驶向中国,而远在墨西哥湾外,

Their banners out across the Mexique Bay.[1]

And in our early days we did the same.
Remembering our fathers in their wreck
We crossed the sea from Palos where they came
And saw, enormous to the little deck,
A shore in silence waiting for a name.

The treasures of Cathay were never found.
In this America, this wilderness
Where the axe echoes with a lonely sound,
The generations labor to possess
And grave by grave we civilize the ground.

---

[1] 哥伦布西航到东方的思想主要来自一部伪经，该书认为陆地西端的西班牙到东端印度的距离极远，而由海路到印度极近。他十年中四次西航，虽登上一些加勒比岛屿和南美大陆，但始终远离北美大陆，至死还认为他到达的是印度附近的岛屿。

那几位船长把他们的旗帜挂上。

在我们早期,我们做同样的事情。
还记得我们的祖先在其破船里,
我们像他们,从帕洛斯渡海远行,
从小甲板上看到极广袤的土地:
这海岸静静地等待着给它命名。

从来就没有找到过中国的宝藏。
而在这亚美利加,这原先的荒野,
现在斧子声在发出寂寞的回响,
而一代一代的劳作挣起了家业:
凭一个个坟墓,我们开化这地方。

WILLIAM BURFORD

A Christmas Tree

Star,

If you are

A love compassionate,

You will walk with us this year.

We face a glacial distance, who are here

Huddld[1]

At your feet.

1　Huddld 是 Huddled 的故意误拼，让人感到拥挤得连字母也挤掉了；译文中用繁体"擁擠"，做法不同却有同样效果。

伯福德(1927—)

圣诞树

星啊

你那爱中

如果含有怜悯,

来年就和我们同行。

这里我们面对冰河距离

拥挤

在你脚底。

PART FOUR

Limericks

第四部分

立马锐克

from A BOOK OF NONSENSE

There was an Old Man with a beard,

Who said, 'It is just as I feared!—

 Two Owls and a Hen,

 Four Larks and a Wren,

Have all built their nests in my beard!'

There was a Young Lady of Ryde,

Whose shoe-strings were seldom untied.

 She purchased some clogs,

 And some small spotted dogs,

And frequently walked about Ryde.

There was an Old Man with a nose,

Who said, 'If you choose to suppose

 That my nose is too long,

 You are certainly wrong!'

The remarkable man with a nose.

There was an Old Man on a hill,

Who seldom, if ever, stood still;

 He ran up and down

 In his grandmother's gown,

Which adorned the Old Man on a hill.

选自《胡调集》

这位老汉有胡须一大把,
他说:"这一点让我害怕——
　　两只鸥䴘一只鸡,
　　四只云雀一只鹪,
都在我胡须里筑窝住下。"

这年轻的女士来自赖德,
她解开鞋带的事很难得。
　　她买了几只小花狗
　　和一些木屐,然后
常常就这样闲逛在赖德。

有位长鼻子老头这样讲:
"谁要是以为我鼻子太长,
　　我就要当面告诉他:
　　你肯定肯定错掉啦!"
这位长鼻子老头不寻常。

这一位是小山上的老汉,
要他站停了不动非常难;
　　他总是上上下下跑,
　　身穿外婆的旧长袍——
这长袍包装这山上老汉。

from THE BABY'S OWN AESOP

1. The Fox and the Grapes

This fox has a longing for grapes,

He jumps, but the bunch still escape.

   So he goes away sour;

   And, 'tis said, to this hour

Declares that he's no taste for grapes.

2. The Cock and the Pearl

A Rooster, while scratching for grain,

Found a pearl. He just paused to explain

   That a jewel's no good

   To a fowl wanting food,

And then kicked it aside with disdain.

3. The Wolf and the Lamb

A Wolf, wanting lamb for his dinner,

Growled out, 'Lamb, you wronged me, you sinner.'

   Bleated Lamb, 'Nay, not true!'

   Answered Wolf, 'Then 't was Ewe—

Ewe or Lamb, you will serve for my dinner.'

选自《宝宝的伊索》

1. 狐狸和葡萄

这狐狸一心要想吃葡萄,
他跳呀蹦呀总是够不到。
　据说在走开的时候,
　他酸溜溜地开了口,
说是没什么胃口吃葡萄。

2. 公鸡和珍珠

公鸡刨着地,找吃的东西,
发现了一颗珍珠却叹息,
　说是他要的是食物,
　珍珠对于他没用处,
随即不屑地往边上一踢。

3. 狼与小羊

狼想把小羊当晚饭,吼道:
"你欺负了我,你这小强盗!"
　小羊咩咩说:"你撒谎!"
　狼叫道:"那么是你娘——
不管谁,你得让我吃个饱。"

4. The Wind and the Sun

The Wind and the Sun had a bet,
The wayfarer's cloak which should get:
   Blew the Wind, the cloak clung;
   Shone the Sun, the cloak flung
Showed the Sun had the best of it yet.

4. 风和太阳

风神和太阳神打了一个赌,
看谁让赶路人脱掉厚衣服。
 风猛吹,厚衣更紧裹;
 太阳晒,厚衣赶紧脱——
到头来,太阳叫风认了输。

from LYRICS PATHETIC & HUMOROUS FROM A TO Z

A was an Afghan Ameer
Who played the accordion by ear.
   When ambassadors called,
   They first listened appalled,
Then would suddenly all disappear.

B was a burly burgrave
Who boasted he bold was and brave.
   But he blushed, it is said,
   Till his beard turned quite red,
So he thought it were better to shave.

C was a cook from Chang-chew
Who once made a crocodile stew.
   But when called by the bell,
   His red pepper-box fell,
So that all he could answer was 'Tchew.'

D was a dignified dame
Who doubtless was not much to blame.
   She played draughts with a lord,
   And was dreadfully bored,
Which occasioned the loss of her game.

选自《谐趣诗 A 到 Z》

A 是埃米尔，主宰阿富汗，
爱凭耳朵把手风琴拉着玩，
　　埃及大使们来拜访，
　　刚一听就暗暗惊慌——
"啊"了声，全都立刻往回转。

B 是膀阔脖子粗的保安官，
他夸口讲自己胆大可包天。
　　但据说不仅脸变红，
　　胡子也变得红彤彤，
他心想，拔了胡子就不难堪。

C 是来自长丘市的厨师，
他曾把鳄鱼熬成了汤汁。
　　忽听到铃响催上菜，
　　匆忙中辣酱翻下来，
吃惊的他脱口应道："该死！"

D 是德高望重的大贵妇，
当然没多少可指责之处；
　　一次同大老爷对局，
　　心底里却大感烦腻，
结果就导致那盘棋大输。

黄杲炘译著年表

英诗汉译(非对照本)

《柔巴依集》(根据原作第四版)上海译文版1982,1991。本书乃第一本拙译英诗,既在英诗汉译中首创"三兼顾"这一迄今最严格的译诗要求,也首先使用原有的准确译名"柔巴依",体现了与维吾尔族等的这种传统诗体一脉相承的关系。

《华兹华斯抒情诗选》上海译文版1986,1988,1990,1992;修订版2000。本书是国内首先出现的华兹华斯专集。

台湾桂冠版繁体字本《华滋华茨抒情诗选》1998。

陕西师大版插图本2016。

司各特《末代行吟诗人之歌》上海译文版1987。本书是该诗最早汉译本,修订后易名《末代行吟人之歌》,收进《英国叙事诗四篇》陕西师大版,2016。

《丁尼生诗选》上海译文版1995。本书是最早的丁尼生汉译本,至今仍是唯一汉译本。

乔叟《坎特伯雷故事》南京译林版插图本1998，非插图本1999，精装本2001。本书以最高得票获第四届全国优秀外国文学图书奖一等奖。

　　台湾猫头鹰版繁体字本2001。

　　上海译文版修订本2007，插图本2011，典藏本2013。

　　台湾远足文化版（上）2012年12月，（下）2013年1月。

　　陕西师大版插图修订本2016。

　　果麦·上海文艺版插图本2019。

《英国叙事诗四篇》（含蒲柏《秀发遭劫记》，司各特《末代行吟人之歌》，丁尼生《伊诺克·阿登》，王尔德《里丁监狱谣》）陕西师大版插图本2016。

《美国抒情诗选》上海译文版1989，1990，1992；增订本2002。本书是我国大陆上第一本涵盖古今的美国诗选。

《英美爱情诗萃》上海译文版（精／平）1992，增订本《恋歌：英美爱情诗萃》2002。

《英国抒情诗选》上海译文版1997。

英汉对照译诗集

《英国抒情诗100首》上海译文版1986，1988，1990，1993；修订本1998。

《美国抒情诗100首》上海译文版1994，2001。学英网(深圳)2000。《文汇读书周报》(1996/2/24)"经理荐书"栏上，两书获上海外文图书公司总经理推荐。

《英语爱情诗一百首》对外翻译版1993，1994，1995，1997……[1]

香港商务版1995。

台湾商务版1995。

《柔巴依一百首》(根据原作第四版)对外翻译版1998。

《柔巴依一百首》(根据原作第一版)湖北教育版插图本2007年1月初印，9月二印。

蒲柏《秀发遭劫记》湖北教育版插图本2007年1月初印，9月二印。

该诗至今仍是国内唯一全译本，已收进《英国叙事诗四篇》。

《英国短诗选》湖北教育版插图本2011。

《美国短诗选》湖北教育版插图本2011。

《英语爱情短诗选》湖北教育版插图本2011。

《英语青春诗选》湖北教育版插图本2011。

《英语十四行诗选》湖北教育版插图本2011。

《英语趣诗选》湖北教育版插图本2011。

《跟住你美丽的太阳——英语爱情诗选》上海译文版2011。

杜拉克诗画集《谐趣诗A~Z》(与下面的《柔巴依集》合一册)安徽人民版彩图本2013。

---

[1] 1997年后未收到重印样书，但两次偶经上海外文书店，先后买到换了封面的《英美爱情诗一百首》和《英语爱情诗一百首》，版权页上都是"2001年1月北京第4次印刷"。

《柔巴依集》(原作第二版，与《谐趣诗 A~Z》合一册) 安徽人民版彩
　　图本 2013。
《丁尼生诗选》外语教学与研究版 2014，2018；馆配本 2014。
《英国名诗选》上海外语教育版 2015，2017。
《美国名诗选》上海外语教育版 2015。2018。
《英文滑稽诗 300 首》陕西师大版，2016。
《柔巴依集》陕西师大版彩图本 2016 。这是该诗第一、二、四版汉译
　　的首个合集。
《谐趣诗集》(含利尔《胡调集》与杜拉克《谐趣诗 A 到 Z》两种诗画
　　彩图本) 外语教学和研究版 2018。
《英文十四行诗集》上海外语教育版 2019。
《英文爱情诗集》上海外语教育版 2019。
《英国短诗集》上海外语教育版 2019。
《美国短诗集》上海外语教育版 2019。
《英文青春诗集》上海外语教育版 2019。
《英文趣诗集》上海外语教育版 2019。
《宝宝的伊索》商务印书馆彩图本 (上海) 2020 。本书是汉语中仅见的
　　两种"诗体伊索"之一。拙译中凡有可能的，都做成对照本，至
　　今已近 30 本。

其他译作

《哈桑奇遇记》(译者署名张俪) 上海译文版 1989。

高尔斯华绥《殷红的花朵》上海译文版 1990(精/平),2001。《文汇读书周报》(1991/1/19)"半月热门书排行榜"五本上榜书中列第二。

南京译林版 2014,有声读物 2018。

陕西师大版 2018。

《鲁滨孙历险记》(含续集) 上海译文版平装本 1997(三次);(换封面) 1998,1999,2000,2001;名著普及本 2001,2002;名著必读 2001,2002(两种共五次);(不含续集)新课标必读 2003;名著文库本 2006,2007(两次),2009;名著精选本 2010,2011,2014(两次),2015,2016,2018;40译文本 2018(两次),2019(两次)。(含续集)精装插图本 1998,1999,2000,2001;(典藏本) 2013;有声读物 2018。

《鲁滨孙历险记》(含续集) 陕西师大修订版插图本 2018。这是坊间仅见的上下合集,也是国内第一个称"历险记"的译本(因为鲁滨孙从未"漂流")。

《拉封丹寓言诗》(法汉对照) 上海译文版 1980。

《拉封丹寓言》(与钱春绮合译) 北岳文艺版插图本 1996。

《拉封丹寓言全集》(与钱春绮合译) 湖北教育版插图本 2007。

陕西师大版插图本 2016。

《伊索寓言》(含 313 则) 北岳文艺版插图本 1996。北岳文艺版私印本

2011。

北京日报版2017。

《伊索寓言》(英汉对照,含338则)湖北教育版插图本2007,2008。

《伊索寓言500则》陕西师大版插图本2016。

《伊索寓言诗365首》陕西师大版插图本2017。本书是汉语中仅见的两种"诗体伊索"之一。

《伊索寓言》(382则,湖北教育版中加44则新译)四川人民版2020。

《宝宝的伊索》(66首"诗体伊索")商务印书馆(上海)插图本2020。

《丽人·拾零集》(含中短篇小说及译诗随笔等),陕西师大版2019。

参译作品

《英美桂冠诗人诗选》上海文艺版1994。

《文学精选:外国诗歌经典》上海译文版1998.

《魔戒》(一译《指环王》)台湾联经版1998。

《王尔德全集·诗歌卷》中国文学版2000等。

著作

文集《从柔巴依到坎特伯雷——英语诗汉译研究》湖北教育版1999。

修订版《英语诗汉译研究——从柔巴依到坎特伯雷》2007。就管见所及，这是第一个有关英诗汉译的个人文集。

《英诗汉译学》上海外语教育版 2007，增订版 2019。本书获中国大学出版社首届优秀学术著作奖一等奖。

文集《译诗的演进》上海译文版 2012。

文集《译路漫漫》陕西师大版 2016。这些文集中的拙文主要发表在《中国翻译》、《外国语》、《诗网络》(香港)、《东方翻译》、《外语与翻译》、《中华读书报》、《文汇读书周报》、《文学报》等报刊。

译著集《丽人拾零集》陕西师大版 2019。

译作中，《坎特伯雷故事》以最高得票获第四届优秀外国文学图书一等奖。

著作中，《英诗汉译学》获中国大学出版社图书奖首届优秀学术著作一等奖。

《中国翻译》(1987 到 2019 共 12 篇)

1987 年第 2 期，《从"鲁拜"谈到"柔巴依"》。

1988 年第 2 期，《理解还是误解——也谈弗罗斯特的小诗"Dust of Snow"》。

1992 年第 5 期，《一种可行的译诗要求——也谈英语格律诗的汉译》。

1999 年第 6 期，《英语格律诗汉译标准的量化及应用》。

2002 年第 5 期，《追求内容与形式的逼真——从看不懂的译诗谈起》。

2003 年第 6 期，《是否有可能"超越"原作——谈英语格律诗的汉译》。

2004年第5期,《菲氏柔巴依是意译还是"形译"?——谈诗体移植及其他》。

2008年第2期,《英诗汉译:发展中的专业》(《英诗汉译学》前言)。

2013年第2期,《突破英诗汉译的"传统"》。

2014年第1期,《非常诗,非常译——谈杜拉克"立马锐克"与"创形-创意翻译》。

2016年第3期,《对闻一多译诗的再认识》。

2019年第1期,《〈老洛伯〉一百岁了——从胡适的"尝试"看译诗发展》。

《外国语》(1991到1996共6篇)

1991年第6期,《从英语"像形诗"的翻译谈格律诗的图形美问题》。

1993年第2期,《译诗者与原诗作者的一次"对抗"》(后用作《英文十四行诗集》前言)。

1993年第4期,《英语爱情诗一百首·前言》(后易名为《诗歌形式的表意功能与译诗中的字数控制问题》)。

1994年第3期,《英诗格律的演化与翻译问题》(《英国抒情诗选》前言)。

1995年第2期,《诗未必是"在翻译中丧失掉的东西"——兼谈汉语在译诗中的优势》。

1996年第4期,《格律诗翻译中的"接轨"问题》。

《外语与翻译》(1998 到 2010 共 10 篇)

1998 年第 2 期,《是巧合,还是剽窃》。

1999 年第 3 期,《英语格律诗汉译标准的量化及应用》。

2001 年第 2 期,《译诗进化的方向:英诗汉译百年回眸》(后易名为《译诗的演进:英语诗汉译百年回眸》)。

2004 年第 2 期,《诗体移植是合理而可行的追求——从胡适的一条译诗"语录"谈起》。

2005 年第 3 期,《译诗像跳高,需要"横杆"——序〈法语诗汉译的模式研究〉》。

2006 年第 2 期,《再谈"三兼顾"诗体移植——答王宝童教授》。

2006 年第 4 期,《"一个译诗问题"的今昔——从徐志摩的探究谈起》。

2007 年第 4 期,《译诗,也要注意常理》。

2009 年第 1 期,《不同的译诗观,不同的结果——答陈凌》。

2010 年第 1 期,《"三兼顾"译法是译诗发展的结果——答张传彪、刘新民》。

《诗网络》(香港)(2003 到 2006 共 5 篇)

2003 年 10 月号,《脱轨的译文:新诗的机车——谈"新其形式"与"中西诗形的结合点"》。

2004 年 6 月号,《诗体移植是合理而可行的追求——从胡适的一条译诗"语录"谈起》。

2004年12月号,《菲氏柔巴依是意译还是"形译"?——谈诗体移植及其他》。

2005年8月号,《译诗像跳高:需要"横杆"——序〈法语诗汉译的模式研究〉》。

2006年2月号,《李尔和麦克斯韦之外》。

《东方翻译》(2011到2019共10篇)

2011年第5期,《也谈怎样译诗——兼答傅浩先生》。

2012年第2期,《从一次征译诗活动想到》。

2014年第5期,《从胡适的白话译诗〈关不住了〉说起》(《美国名诗选》前言)。

2016年第1期,《洛威尔一节诗的中国故事》。

2016年第3期,《从〈伊索寓言〉说起》。

2017年第5期,《"立马锐克"与我的缘分》。

2018年第1期,《也谈"十九行二韵体诗"的翻译》。

2018年第4期,《谈译诗的形式》。

2019年第4期,《语体译诗百年缩影——聚焦于一首四行诗》。

2019年第5期,《告别翻译》。

《中学生阅读》(高中版，1997 到 2001 共 5 篇)

1997 年第 11 期，华兹华斯的《华兹华斯抒情诗选》。
1998 年第 7 期，笛福的《鲁滨孙历险记》。
1999 年第 7 期，丁尼生的《丁尼生诗选》。
2000 年第 10 期，乔叟的《坎特伯雷故事》。
2001 年第 2 期，《书，是一种路标》。

《世界之窗》

2001 年第 1 期，《美国历史最悠久的女子高校——霍尔约克山学院点滴》。
2001 年第 6 期，《没去走的路》。

《现代外语》

1997 年第 1 期，《诗歌翻译是否"只分坏和次坏的两种"——兼谈汉字在译诗中的优势》。

《诗刊》

2007 年 6 月号(上)，《要读什么样的译诗》。

《文学评论》(香港)

2014年10月号,《世事沧桑心未冷——王伟明与黄杲炘细谈翻译》。

《新民晚报》

1982年3月28日,《〈柔巴依集〉传奇》。
1996年11月18日,《鲁滨孙漂流过没有?》。
1997年11月24日,《英诗的精译本》。

《文汇读书周报》(1994到2017共11篇)

1994年10月29日,《初会丁尼生》。
2000年3月4日,《诗究竟是否可译》。
2000年9月30日,《译诗的进化》(整版)。
2001年1月20日,《华兹华斯的抒情歌谣》。
2002年8月2日,《寻图记》。
2003年5月16日,《"柔巴依"的有趣发现》。
2007年4月23日,《美轮美奂柔巴依》(整版)。
2007年10月26日,《"柔巴依"与"鲁拜"》。
2011年7月8日,《经典创作的经典制作:〈坎特伯雷故事〉中的经典插图》(整版)。

2013年7月26日,《杜拉克的谐趣诗和插图》(整版)。
2017年2月6日,《我的"柔巴依"之路》(整版)。

《文汇报·笔会》

2000年12月3日,《请英国诗歌之父作证》。
2001年3月31日,《谁过滤了鲁滨孙》。

《文学报》

2004年1月29日,《脱轨的译文:新诗的机车——谈"新其形式"与"中西诗形的结合点"》。
2005年6月23日,《格律未必是束缚》。
2013年8月8日,"新批评",《诗,未必不可译》(整版)。
2020年5月28日,"新批评"《从伊索寓言出发》(整版)(《索伊寓言诗365首》前言)。

《大公报》(香港)

2004年11月21日,《一本美丽的书——〈法国诗选〉印象》。

2005年7月3日,《从奥登和菲尔德想到》。

2006年4月9日,《一首外国诗的故事》。

2007年6月17日,《诺顿夫人的一首短诗》。

《中华读书报·国际文化》(2014到2019共10篇)

2014年4月16日,《〈英诗十三味〉的异味》。

2014年10月15日,《从胡适第一首白话译诗〈老洛伯〉说起》(整版)(《英国名诗选》前言)。

2015年6月24日,《把"丧失掉的东西"还给译诗》。

2015年12月2日,《〈柔巴依集〉的中国故事——英诗汉译百年发展与出版的见证》(整版)。

2016年4月6日,《格律体新诗和英语格律诗——从穆旦一节诗谈起》(整版)。

2016年9月21日,《话说伊索寓言的诗体汉译》(《伊索寓言诗365首》前言)。

2017年9月6日,《"立马锐克"的中国故事》(整版)。

2018年6月20日,《闻一多:格律移植的先驱》(整版)。

2018年11月7日,《格律诗的无限可能——从"来自大英图书馆的珍宝"说起》。

2019年3月20日,《从剑桥纪念徐志摩说起》(整版)。

《世界文学》

1983年第6期,《偷牛贼》(诗,外二首),作者【加拿大】波琳·约翰逊。

《译文丛刊》

1983年4月(次年10月重印)诗歌特辑《在大海边》,译诗31首(美、法、德作者)。

1984年3月专辑《国际笔会作品集》,译诗7首(英、美作者)。

1985年7月诗歌特辑《春天最初的微笑》,译诗5篇(爱尔兰、加拿大、美国作者)。

1985年12月专辑《国际笔会作品集》,《波盖尔先生》(中篇小说),作者【美】布思·塔金顿。

1988年9月,《丽人》(中篇小说),作者【美】布思·塔金顿。

《百花洲》

1986年第3期,《梅斯维尔镇的歌手》(短篇小说),作者【美】林·拉德纳。

《美国文学丛刊》

1983 年第 3 期,《夜总会》(短篇小说),作者【美】凯瑟玲·布勒许。
1984 年第 1 期,《觉醒:一段回忆》(散文),作者【美】阿纳·邦当。

《外国故事》

1994 年第 5 期,《煞基船长》(短篇小说),作者【英】柯南·道尔。
1995 年第 5 期,《黑豹眼睛》(短篇小说),作者【美】安布罗斯·比尔斯。
1995 年第 6 期,《空中骑手》(短篇小说),作者【美】安布罗斯·比尔斯。

《译文》

2001 年第二辑,《400 米自由泳 /400-Meter Freestyle》(诗),作者【美】玛克莘·库敏。
2002 年第一辑,《早餐的奇迹》(诗),作者【美】伊丽莎白·毕晓普。

图书在版编目（CIP）数据

我得重下海去：黄杲炘译诗自选集：汉英对照 / 黄杲炘译著. -- 北京：中译出版社，2021.9
（我和我的翻译 / 罗选民主编）
ISBN 978-7-5001-6701-3

Ⅰ. ①我… Ⅱ. ①黄… Ⅲ. ①世界文学—作品综合集—汉、英②黄杲炘—译文—文集—汉、英 Ⅳ. ①I11

中国版本图书馆CIP数据核字(2021)第134997号

出版发行	中译出版社
地　　址	北京市西城区车公庄大街甲4号物华大厦六层
电　　话	（010）68359827，68359303（发行部）；68359725（编辑部）
传　　真	（010）68357870
邮　　编	100044
电子邮箱	book@ctph.com.cn
网　　址	http://www.ctph.com.cn
策划编辑	范祥镇　刘瑞莲
责任编辑	范祥镇　王诗同
装帧设计	秋　萍
排　　版	冯　兴
印　　刷	北京顶佳世纪印刷有限公司
经　　销	新华书店
规　　格	880毫米×1230毫米　1/32
印　　张	12.625
字　　数	295千字
版　　次	2021年9月第1版
印　　次	2021年9月第1次

ISBN 978-7-5001-6701-3　　　　定价：65.00元

版权所有　侵权必究
中译出版社